# VIOLENCE

A NOVEL

# CE

# 101

## DENIS WRIGHT

G. P. Putnam's Sons

AN IMPRINT OF PENGUIN GROUP (USA) INC.

G. P. PUTNAM'S SONS
A DIVISION OF PENGUIN YOUNG READERS GROUP.
Published by The Penguin Group. Penguin Group (USA) Inc., 375 Hudson Street, New York, NY 10014, U.S.A. Penguin Group (Canada), 90 Eglinton Avenue East, Suite 700, Toronto, Ontario M4P 2Y3, Canada (a division of Pearson Penguin Canada Inc.). Penguin Books Ltd, 80 Strand, London WC2R 0RL, England. Penguin Ireland, 25 St. Stephen's Green, Dublin 2, Ireland (a division of Penguin Books Ltd.). Penguin Group (Australia), 250 Camberwell Road, Camberwell, Victoria 3124, Australia (a division of Pearson Australia Group Pty Ltd). Penguin Books India Pvt Ltd, 11 Community Centre, Panchsheel Park, New Delhi—110 017, India. Penguin Group (NZ), 67 Apollo Drive, Rosedale, North Shore 0632, New Zealand (a division of Pearson New Zealand Ltd). Penguin Books (South Africa) (Pty) Ltd, 24 Sturdee Avenue, Rosebank, Johannesburg 2196, South Africa. Penguin Books Ltd, Registered Offices: 80 Strand, London WC2R 0RL, England.

First published in New Zealand by Penguin Group (NZ) in 2007.
First American edition, 2010.

Printed in the United States of America.

Design by Richard Amari.
Text set in Candida Roman.
Library of Congress Cataloging-in-Publication Data is available upon request.

ISBN 978-0-399-25493-2
1   3   5   7   9   10   8   6   4   2

To all the teenage boys I have taught over the years

# 101 FOREWORD

Regarding the story:

Although *Violence 101* is set in New Zealand, it is likely there are Hamish Grahams in every society. He is a highly intelligent boy from a middle-class family, has had every opportunity to be a success, yet he simply doesn't fit the prescribed model. Hamish is seething with anger at his inability to understand the world he inhabits and the inability of those in charge to understand him. He would have loved to have been born in an era when ruthless courage and calculating intelligence were held in high regard, and this is why he takes refuge with past military heroes like Alexander the Great.

Hamish is able to justify his antisocial violence with

ease, but I don't want him to be labeled as sociopath, psychopath or genius. These labels are very broad and can often prevent genuine attempts to understand individual cases. The inability of societies worldwide to identify and understand troubled children can and does have very serious consequences.

Regarding the setting:

In New Zealand, the Maori people are the *Tangata Whenua* (first people of the land). These natives formed a complex and tightly regulated tribal society, the basis of which is centered on ownership and protection of land and tribal *mana*, or honor. I believe there are many similarities to how Native Americans lived prior to European settlement.

In 1769 Captain James Cook charted New Zealand's coastline. Admiring the natives and seeing the huge potential for British settlement, Cook claimed the land for the English crown, and the first Europeans arrived late in the eighteenth century. In the initial decades of contact, Maori and European settlers got on reasonably well and conflicts over land were relatively small. Maori were very keen to acquire European tools, but they also rapidly saw the tribal warfare benefits of acquiring guns and this had devastating results for those tribes that were not able to do so.

In 1840, the Treaty of Waitangi was signed between Maori tribal leaders and the English crown, promising the Maori ownership of their lands and resources in return for British protection and sovereignty of the country. But a huge influx of British settlers led to fights and squabbles over land breaking out. The land wars of the 1860s were a dark period of New Zealand history and the scars are still there today. Between 1860 and 1890, most of the remaining communal Maori land was lost by breaking it up into individual titles, and allowing its sale to Europeans.

Alienation from tribal lands, combined with little natural resistance to European diseases, had a devastating impact on Maori and numbers went into serious decline. By the turn of the twentieth century, many people thought that Maori were literally a dying race. However, due to intensive health and education initiatives, numbers recovered and Maori now make up about seventeen percent of the New Zealand population of four and a half million. New Zealand also has a considerable Polynesian community—approximately 400,000—most of whom are from the Samoan Islands.

In the last thirty years there has been a resurgence of Maori cultural awareness, both from Maori and *Pakeha* (European New Zealanders). Maori language (*Te Reo Maori*) holds equal status with English as an official language of New Zealand and most New Zealanders are at least familiar with basic vocabulary.

This is not to say that Maori enjoy the same socioeconomic status as Pakeha New Zealanders. Sadly, Maori and Polynesians make up large numbers in unemployment figures, educational underachievement and prison numbers. However, these issues are not swept under the carpet, and raising Maori educational achievement and general living conditions is a cornerstone of New Zealand's political and educational systems.

—Denis Wright

# 101
## PART
## ONE *Arrival*

# 101
# CHAPTER ONE

The management staff of Manukau New Horizons Boys'
Home waited in a cramped office and fidgeted. There
were four of them, with an empty chair waiting for a fifth.
The principal, Helen Grenville, looked at her watch for
the third time in as many minutes. Eight fifteen and Terry
Swanson was late again. If Helen didn't start the weekly
meeting very soon, the others would drift off, and Monday was such a busy day. She cleared her throat to begin
speaking, and in he breezed.

"Sorry all, not holding you up, am I?" Terry slid into
his chair and dragged his papers out of a battered leather
satchel.

"No more than you do every Monday, Terry," Helen replied tightly, "and there's just so much to do today."

"Mea culpa, humble apologies, et cetera, et cetera. Come on, let's not dillydally. What's up, Helen?"

She suppressed the reply he deserved and started the meeting.

"Good morning, everyone. Thank you to those who were on time. You may be aware by now that we had somewhat of an emergency on Friday afternoon in the carving class." Helen looked pointedly at Toko Wihongi. The leanly muscled physical education instructor and ex–army sergeant wore a mask of indifference. "It seems that Charlie Harris, the new carving tutor contracted by Toko, objected to being called a fat nigger by Raymond Maihi and thought near strangulation might bring the boy to his senses." Multiple voices cut in at once, but Helen continued loudly. "At which point Junior Thompson and several others began throwing chisels around the workshop, one of which bounced off a wall and almost severed Alex Mason's ear. End result? Alex has six stitches in his left ear, Raymond has severe bruising of the larynx and Charlie Harris is in breach of his contract."

Terry jumped in before the others. "And now you want us to abandon the carving classes, right?"

"Well, for goodness' sake. We put ten boys in there, all with histories of violence, and arm them with lethal weapons. Is that a wise thing to do, Terry?"

"Oh come on, Helen, the boys love carving and for once we're teaching them some genuinely useful skills. These things just happen sometimes and—"

"What happened," cut in Toko, "was that Charlie was put into the class unsupervised. The policy is very clear for all tutors. No tutor, especially a new one, is to take any sort of practical class without at least one experienced supervisor. Just because Charlie is large and Maori doesn't mean he can wave a magic wand with those kids. You all know that. We stuffed up, not Charlie. We were in breach of the tutors' contract, not Charlie. I'll speak to him again, but we just have to make sure that he has assistance at all times. In fact, I'll stay with him myself this week."

Helen sighed and brushed a hand through her short gray hair.

"Thank you, Toko. You're right, of course. It's just so . . . Anyway, we need to move on. Item number two on the agenda is a new placement, Hamish Graham, a fourteen-year-old Pakeha from Wellington. And yes, I am aware that we are at overflow, but Warburton can no longer deal with him, and Rongomoana flatly refuses to take him. That leaves good old us. Anyway, here are his profile sheets. I'll shut up while you read."

She sat back and watched her staff as they skim-read the profile. The first to speak was Sarah Quinn, the bubbly young therapist from Wellington.

"Hey, this is the boy who drowned that old Iraqi chap in Miramar a couple of years ago. Remember? The papers and TV were full of it. Lots of stories about him being some sort of cold-blooded killer. Wow—so we have him now, eh?"

"Yes, it seems we do," Helen replied. "By all accounts he's extremely intelligent, IQ through the roof. We should put him on correspondence courses immediately. Before he went to Warburton, he attended high school for a term, where he was in Year Nine. Warburton suggested we put him on Level Three history and classical studies. You'll see that he's also very good at math and physics. Right, well, he starts on Wednesday and I suppose we'll find out a lot more about him then. Item three is—"

"Um, Helen?" asked Simon Whittle, the dour second in command. "This profile leaves out some important details, don't you think? Hmm? I mean, just why is young master Graham no longer welcome at Warburton? Why won't Rongomoana take him, and why the unholy haste to move him here? What exactly has he done?"

Helen had expected these questions and replied to them in a neutral monotone.

"It seems he victimized several of the staff, culminating in him trying to gouge out the eyes of one of his therapists, Milly Polachovic—some of you may know her. She had apparently laughed at him during a therapy session—something about him trying to sexually harass her. Milly suffered serious damage to the cornea of her right eye and moderate damage to her left. Oh, and he broke her nose. So there you have it. He arrives Wednesday afternoon at three. Simon, you are more than welcome to join me in the initial interview. And by the way, Terry—he's on your caseload."

## Journal Entry 1—May 10

I am fourteen years and five months old. My name is Hamish Graham and this is the journal I have to write. Doesn't worry me because I'm a good writer and I'd rather write than talk any day, although I like talking to Terry. The people who run this place don't know what to make of me. Just like the last place I was in. I hope these people are a bit better than the retards running Warburton. What a bunch of morons! If I want to talk, I'll talk, and if I don't, I won't. Mostly I don't. Writing this journal is Mrs. Grenville's genius (yeah right) way of starting my "rehabilitation." She's even given me my own laptop. She said my audience is whoever I want it to be. I pretended I didn't want to, but I like writing. It's easy and everyone says I'm good at it. The work (joke) in these boys' homes is too simple for me, so once again I'll be the only boy here doing proper lessons through the Correspondence School. I suppose I'll be a historian, a philosopher or maybe a physicist when I'm older. So here is my journal to whoever wants to read it.

Most of the other boys in this place are thick-as-pig-shit losers from crap families. They should be easy meat for the legions of therapists and social workers who try to fix us broken-down kids. (*Legion* is a good word from Terry, originally meaning "a body of between 3,000 to 6,000 Roman soldiers.") Most of the loser kids here are easy to fix. I don't know why everyone reckons it's so hard. Most people are too soft on them. They need a good feed, strict discipline, heaps of exercise and heaps of attention. A year in the army would sort most of them out. The main thing is they need to be taken away from their crap, loser families. Families are way overrated. It really bugs me that almost all the out-of-it kids I come across in these boys' homes are eventually returned to their loser families, when we all know that they are the cause of their problems in the first place.

In my first term of high school a science "teacher" didn't know how to deal with me in the classroom, where it was fairly obvious to her and the other students that I should have been teaching the class, not her. I would have kept better discipline for a start! To shut me up, she had the idea of letting me do my own science research project. I said I would do a project on some aspect of population control. All good so far, but the shit really hit the fan when I presented it to her and the class. She had the cheek to psych at me big-time for writing a perfectly sensible project about introducing a License to Breed scheme. My carefully researched proposal was that contraceptives should be put into New Zealand's water supply and that people who wanted to have a baby would have to apply to a Central Breeding Authority (CBA) to see if they were suitable to raise kids. If suitable, they would be given a "birthing pill," which would temporarily neutralize the effect of the contraceptives in the water. In my project I included some possible test questions to ensure parents had a reasonable level of intelligence. The teacher said I was a racist because including questions on calculus and physics in such a test would mean very few Polynesian or Maori babies would be born. What the hell? She was the racist, not me. I never mentioned anything about race! I patiently tried to explain to her and the class a little about the science of eugenics and about how it got bad press because of the Nazis, who, like most people, misunderstood the beauty of the system. It is not for creating some sort of master race. The idea is to make child rearing a serious social responsibility and not an automatic right. Good eugenics creates a reasonable balance of cultures and socioeconomic levels while ensuring that those who are unsuitable to breed don't and that unwanted congenital illnesses are eventually bred out of a population base. Think of how many social problems we would solve by not letting losers breed more losers. Seems every time you look at the news or read a paper, you see hordes of losers staring at you, with the same defeated expressions. Sometimes they put on a bit of a show for the cameras and give a gang salute or something equally moronic, but it doesn't hide the fact that mostly they're just sad, dumb losers. I told the teacher that in my scheme, she definitely would have failed the breeding test and that she must have found her teaching certificate in a cereal box. I think I was sent out of class then—what an overreaction! So anyway, we seem to be stuck with all these loser kids.

I think we should have these special schools for bad kids in hard-core places like Waiouru and Central

Otago. They'd do school subjects from 8:00 a.m. to 1:00 p.m. and then in the afternoon do things like compulsory mountain climbing and river crossing while wearing huge packs. The kids who refuse to participate would get fed bread and water until they changed their minds. I would divide them into various teams and have mock wars. Military history would be a compulsory subject. I would also make the study of violence compulsory.

Seems to me all good things come from violence in one way or another. Do you know why the ancient Greek and Roman cultures had the time and leisure to sit around thinking up all sorts of clever philosophical ideas and inventing all sorts of neat stuff like flush toilets and aqueducts? Through violence, that's how. Those so-called cultured societies needed huge armies to keep invaders at bay and to capture slaves and resources from other places. Slaves did the hard work, and most of them were treated like crap. I bet you didn't know that the ancient Romans had a subterranean aqueduct system about four hundred kilometers long. Thousands of laborers, most of whom were slaves, worked under the direction of the *curator aquarum* to keep it maintained. They were so well made that Rome still uses a lot of them today.

The threat of massive violence allowed those societies to do other neat stuff like design hard-core buildings and compose music and write plays. Heaps of great inventions in more modern times came about because of war as well. Things like barbed wire, bulldozers and four-wheel-drive vehicles were first used in war, and look how beneficial those three inventions have been to the farming industry in this country. In fact, I don't know why so many people are scared of celebrating violence, especially when they deal with the boys in these homes. The people who run these boys' homes say that most of us are here because of some sort of violent behavior, but once we are here, rather than seriously getting into the issue, violence is treated as a taboo subject.

Last year I wrote to the minister of education and told him that the New Zealand curriculum should include a compulsory subject called the Psychology of Violence. I wrote a suggested course outline and a sample Level 1 achievement standard (internally assessed—three credits) for a course called Violence 101. The curriculum was kind of like philosophy and political science for dummies, mixed with a study of the world's greatest military strategists, such as Xerxes, Alexander the Great and Genghis Khan, and a bunch of interesting case studies of various mass murderers, like Idi Amin, Pol Pot and Slobodan Milosevic. The minister probably filed my letter straight in the bin or maybe only read the first five or six pages because the reply I got was the standard sort of flunky letter thanking me for my interest in the education system and assuring me that he would pass on my interesting ideas to the relevant curriculum people at the Ministry of Education (translation: go away and stop bothering me, you screwed-up nutter). I wrote him another letter telling him that he, or the flunky who had replied to me, was obviously far too stupid to understand the far-reaching implications of my letter and that the substandard education system of this country is probably a fair reflection of his dangerously low IQ. I didn't get a reply to that letter.

Anyway, before I got sidetracked, I was talking about special tough schools for bad kids. I reckon they would love them. A lot of the bad kids I have come across in boys' homes may be fairly dumb, but they give life a decent shot. They usually aren't the spoiled little mommies' boys who spend half their sad lives playing childish computer games. Well, there are a few decent games, such as World of Warcraft, which I am, of course, a master at playing.

Don't know if bad girls would be into my tough schools, but most girls are good anyway, even the bad ones. Actually, I have come across a couple of genuinely bad girls, and to be honest, they were really interesting people. You hear a lot these days about how loads of girls are going off the rails and doing weird, hard-core violent stuff like bad boys do. That's crap. Sure, some girls are doing violent stuff, but almost all come from loser families and their behavior is fairly boring and predictable. In places like New Zealand there's all this social conditioning to make girls behave in a certain way. You know, be caring and cooperative and sort of soft, but also be hardworking and independent. Most girls are like this. By bad girls I mean the girls who have no apparent reason to lose the plot—girls who come from decent families and who go through all the right conditioning but who still come out with a vicious streak. Bit like me, I suppose.

When I was at intermediate school, I knew these very cool twin girls who were really bad, Melanie and Laura. They came from a good family and were ultra-pretty and all that, but they kept to themselves and were sort of wild and unpredictable. One thing about them is they were both quite physically well developed for twelve-year-olds. They gave this one smartarse boy a big-time bash because he pulled one of their bra straps and made a smart remark about the size of their boobs. They got stuck into him as a team and really messed him up. Man, I was super-impressed. They knew how to punch properly, you know, leading from the shoulder and keeping your wrist rigid. Good job. To tell the truth, I had a big-time crush on them but didn't have a clue what to do about it. Once, I was sitting outside the principal's office waiting to be suspended for some very minor incident with a craft knife, which is so boring I can't bring myself to tell you about it. Anyway, while I was sitting there in my usual seat, the twins arrived, escorted by a couple of red-faced teachers. They were plonked down beside me and instructed not to move until their mother came to collect them. I am very rarely lost for words, but I was this time. I eventually blurted out that I liked the way they gave the bully kid the bash. This went down okay and Melanie said that they had seen me lose my rag at the bus stop after school one day and that they had copied some of my fight moves. Phew! High praise. So we were getting on like a house on fire. We got chatting about other stuff and I was quite impressed at their smartness. Things were progressing well. Then I kind of blew it. I said that maybe I could phone them and the three of us could get it together on the weekend.

Melanie looked me in the eye and said, "In your dreams, dickhead!" I tried to explain that I didn't mean what they must have thought I meant, but this seemed to make it worse. Laura said I was just like the rest of the boys and I should go fuck myself! Talk about knockdown. I still liked them, though, but after that only from a safe distance. Just as well, really, because to tell you the truth, I am useless at getting on with girls. Whatever I say seems to piss them off big-time, especially if I am giving them healthy criticism. Yeah, girls are way too sensitive. Laura and Melanie reminded me a bit of these hardout twin girls called the Ingham twins, who were nationally famous for a while because they were a total law unto themselves. I kept a scrapbook on them when I was little, until my mother threw it out, saying it was an unhealthy obsession. Shows what she knows!

Apparently I am "highly dysfunctional." I really like that word, and Terry and I use it as a joke whenever we talk. He calls me the Dysfunctional Kid. *Dys* is such a great prefix. I could write this entire journal entry on the words *legion* and *dysfunctional,* but that wouldn't count with Mrs. Grenville and I would have to write another entry. She only wants me to write about things that have happened to me or things I have done. She didn't like my real first journal entry because it was about

Alexander the Great and not about me. I was very angry at first because it was all about his campaigns and was really well written. I thought seriously about smashing her one in her big, red smiling mouth. She got a bit scared then and started saying how it was really very good, but that she was more interested in me than Alexander the Great. She made a hilarious (not) joke and said, "Tell me about Hamish the Great." I calmed down a bit then because I realized that she was definitely far too stupid to have understood about Alexander's campaigns anyway. I mean, how could someone as average as her understand anything about the greatest military leader of all time? I felt better after thinking that and the noise in my head went away.

The other boys here are just like the boys in the last place I was in. They swagger around the facility in little gangs, eyeballing other little gangs and getting into arguments and fights over dumb crap. Then there's counseling and everything's "sweet-as, bro" until the next fight. I caused a big-ass fight the day I arrived. Martin, my main social worker from the last place, said it would be a good idea if I was put by myself for a while and then gradually introduced to the other boys, but Mrs. Grenville said that in her opinion, introducing me gradually would set me apart too much and the boys would make it harder for me to settle in. She said that she and her staff would look after me very carefully and ensure I came to no harm. She only smiled when Martin said it was the other boys he was worried about. She looked at me and saw a tall, thin, blue-eyed white boy with a shy smile.

At teatime that night a big, tough Maori boy named Victor knocked a whole glass of milk into my plate of lasagna, accidentally on purpose, when he was reaching for the bread. "Oh, sorry, bro, your glass got in the way." He looked at his mates and laughed in that stupid way boys like him always laugh and didn't see me pick up my fork and drive it hard into his face. It was pretty amazing because it actually stuck in his cheek and hung there for a bit before falling out. Then I punched him two or three times as fast and hard as I could before the other boys jumped on me and we all sort of rolled around yelling and hitting each other, until we were pulled apart by an ultra-strong and intense guy called Mr. Wihongi I think. It was great. Lots of blood and shouting, but no one really hurt much—apart from Victor, who had to go to hospital for a suspected broken nose. I was careful to use the heel of my hand and not my fist—that's always a big mistake because broken knuckles take ages to heal and anyway, with the heel of your hand you can drive in and up at the same time—particularly effective on noses. After that, the boys, even the loser I stuck the fork into, wanted me to be their friend. As if!

Anyway, Mrs. Grenville (you can't call her Helen) and the others who run the place (first names usually, except for Mr. Wihongi, who is some sort of fitness freak PE teacher) are really concerned about me. I don't seem to fit into any of the mad and bad categories they have. They don't know how "such an intelligent boy from such a good home" can be so violent. *Callous* is the word Mrs. Grenville used. I don't like that word much. It makes me think of a ferret or weasel for some reason. There are just some words I like and there are some words I don't like.

I explained to her and the other counselors after the fork incident that violence can be a perfectly rational human reaction to abnormal circumstances. I told them that without violence, mankind would never have made it beyond the caves, and once out of the caves, people unwilling to use violence would not have survived five minutes. I won that argument so easily. The best bit was when I asked Mrs. Grenville if her father or grandfather had ever fought in a war and she said that her father had fought in Egypt and Italy during World War Two. I said that all war is violence. She didn't like me using this line of argument because she said World War Two was a different thing altogether because it was a "just war." Yeah right! I told her that histories are always written by the winners and who the hell is the judge of whether a war is "just" or not? I told her that Victor and his mates would have teased me mercilessly for weeks, if not months, and so sticking a fork in his face and breaking his nose was a very rational solution. They should have been very pleased that I had limited the problem to one incident rather than let it go on for months.

The counselors still wanted to argue with me so I pointed out that the world's greatest leaders have often been extremely violent people and cleverly countered the idea that these leaders weren't personally violent by asking, "So it's okay if minions (one of Terry's greatest words) do the violence for you? Like dropping the bombs on Hiroshima and Nagasaki?" They STILL wanted to continue the discussion so I told them that popular sports like rugby and boxing are built around violence and that James Bond personally kills an average of twenty-seven people per film and that James Bond movies are always blockbusters. I got totally bored with the discussion because I knew that I had won, but they just wanted to keep on going, just so that they wouldn't look dumb. Too late. They looked dumb anyway.

I am exceptionally good at getting rid of counselors I don't want to work with. In the last place I was in, there was this fat American hippie counselor with a very large chest. She used to go on and on about my childhood and "releasing stuff" and "letting go." She even tried to get me to do this special breathing nonsense to expel "bad energy." She couldn't accept that there was no problem with my childhood and I just got really sick of her going on and on with her up-and-down voice and stupid smile. One day I started staring at her chest, as if I had just noticed that she robbed a tit bank or something. She tried to ignore my staring but eventually folded her arms and told me that I was making her feel very uncomfortable. I continued staring directly at her chest until she sort of psyched big-time and yelled that I was sexually harassing her. I looked up at her fat sweaty face and said that the thought of doing anything remotely sexual with her made me want to vomit. She ran from the room crying and that was the last I saw of her.

The only person here who treats me with any kind of respect is Terry. I think he's some sort of child psychologist. The good thing is we hardly ever talk about me but just interesting stuff like Alexander the Great, war-hero Charles Upham, the Trojan War, Maori chief Te Rauparaha, space rockets and various other cool inventions like giant war catapults, oil-drilling platforms and space stations.

Terry is about thirty and has several tattoos and seven piercings, which look stupid on someone his age. I told him this the first time we met and he kind of smiled and said, "Shit, remind me never to show you all my other ones. You'll think I'm a total plonker!" I then pointed out that they made him look gay and he just smiled and said, "Fair enough, Hamish, but what's your point?"

So he's okay. Terry doesn't feel he has to prove that he's as smart as me, but he does have a great vocabulary and we play this funny kind of game where we both know that at some stage in the discussion, he'll throw in a word to die for. I keep a special notebook for all Terry's words and I have arranged it like a personal dictionary. I actually know most of them anyway, but sometimes he comes up with one I don't know, like *minion.* The first word he gave me was *aberration.* In our first meeting he said that I was "a very interesting aberration." Last time we talked, I thought he wasn't going to give me a word. But just when he was leaving, he said, "Okay, mate, that's enough obfuscating for one day. I've got to go and earn my pay now." I never ask him what they mean and he never explains, but I make sure I use the word correctly the next time we meet. That's part of the game. Very cool.

I know Mrs. Grenville will be getting cross reading this stuff about words. She will think I am obfuscating—avoiding writing about stuff she wants to read about, like why I do certain things—but I said to her that if I can't write about some interesting things, then I won't write anything at all. So stuff it! Here is a very short piece on Alexander the Great's childhood (the last stuff I wrote was mostly about his campaigns). If anyone comments on this, I will not write one more word in this stupid journal. I am writing about Alexander for me and Terry, not for you, Mrs. Grenville. Definitely do not let Mr. Whittle read it either.

## Alexander the Great's Childhood

Alexander was born in 356 BC in Pella, the capital of a kingdom in ancient Greece called Macedonia. His father was King Philip II and his mother was Olympias. His parents were very powerful and strong-willed people and they both recognized similar qualities in Alexander from an early age. His parents claimed to be descended from mythical Greek heroes—Philip from Heracles and Olympias from Achilles. Imagine actually believing that! No wonder Alexander acted more and more like some sort of invincible god when he became a man.

Alexander's father created a large and very strong army and turned Macedonia into the strongest state in all of Greece, but all this wasn't just going to fall into Alexander's hands automatically. His father married six times and had numerous sons, so Alexander had to do something special to gain attention.

One day a horse dealer offered the king a huge black stallion for the massive price of 78,000 drachmas. A skilled worker earned about 1,000 drachmas a year, so you can see how much the horse was worth. If you convert that into today's money, the horse would be worth millions. Despite the price, Philip was very interested in the horse, but there was a problem—it was utterly wild and wouldn't let anyone near it. It had only recently killed an experienced horseman who tried to ride him and it lashed out at anyone who approached. Alexander knew that he had a golden opportunity to really impress his father, so he seized the moment and in front of the king and all the other dignitaries he slowly approached the horse. People gasped in fright;

surely the foolish boy would be slashed to death by the razor-sharp hooves. When Alexander reached the stallion, he slowly turned its large head toward the sun and began whispering in its ear and stroking it. When the horse was settled, he leapt on its back and rode it out to the grassy plains and back again at a full gallop.

What the others didn't realize was that Alexander had studied this horse for some time and found out that it had a strong fear of its own large shadow, so turning its head to the sun meant it wouldn't be spooked by the black shapes on the ground. But imagine the courage needed to do that, and in front of the king. Philip was so impressed he bought the horse, named Bucephalus, and gave it to his son. The two were inseparable for almost twenty years of traveling and fighting, and when his great equine friend was finally killed in the Battle of Hydaspes, near a river in modern-day Pakistan, he gave the war-scarred old stallion a full military funeral.

The only other really close friends he had were Hephaestion, a school friend from his days under the direction of Aristotle, and a Persian boy called Bagoas, whom he met in 330 BC. Hephaestion was Alexander's main bodyguard, principal adviser and eventually the grand vizier of the empire, a sort of top administrator.

I would have loved to have had a best friend like

Hephaestion, a comrade in arms, but it never seemed to work out. The boys who were as daring and brave as me were always too dumb, and the boys who were as bright as me were always too weak and cowardly. I once suggested to a clever boy at primary school that we become blood brothers by cutting our palms and clasping hands so our blood mingled. He thought this sounded like a great idea, until I put the plan into action. I had this razor blade and cut my palm with it, but the coward wouldn't let me cut his palm and ran away crying. When I eventually caught him, I held him down and just cut him a little bit and tried to join our blood, but of course the teachers misunderstood the whole thing and I got suspended. Overreaction plus!

Unfortunately I seem to have been born in the wrong time period and most people hate the way I behave and the way I think. This is why I daydream about Alexander and the times he lived in so much. Back then people valued ruthlessness, intelligence and reckless bravery. Back then boys were trained to be real men, not politically correct little mommies' boys.

I am going to stop writing about Alexander now because sometimes it makes me quite depressed coming back to reality, just like when you have been to a very cool movie and then you have to walk out of the theater into your regular life. When I came out of the Embassy Theatre in Wellington after watching the first Lord of the Rings movie, I got so depressed that I couldn't face getting on the dumb bus and looking at all the stupid, boring people and so ended up walking all the way back home to Wadestown, which took an hour and a half.

# 101
# CHAPTER
# TWO

Helen Grenville sat hunched over a copy of Hamish's first journal entry.

"So, what do you make of him, Terry? I mean he's certainly taken a big shine to you since you appear to be the *only* one here who treats him with any kind of respect and the rest of us are all so average and stupid."

Terry smiled. "He's a great judge of character, eh? Seriously, though, this boy is a one-off. I've been in this game for over ten years now and I've never encountered a kid remotely like him. Look at the size of his first journal entry—bet you didn't imagine he would write this much! Mind you, I've seen him on that laptop of his— touch-typing and damn near mistake free! He's very intelligent and incredibly well read for a fourteen-year-old. Shit, he's read more than most intelligent adults. And how about his turn of phrase? A really weird mix of formal language and slang. He also seems capable of a high degree of self-analysis. Most boys here operate on an 'I fight, therefore I am' philosophy, whereas old Hamish has very little interest in fighting for the sake of fighting."

Helen shook her head. "Are you kidding me? His professed heroes are all fighting men, and look at the way he dealt with Victor Kaiarahi. And that bit about using the heel of the hand. Now that was downright savage."

"I wasn't there at the time, but by all accounts he was quite calm about it all. I think he genuinely saw it as a rational thing to do in the circumstances."

"Or is that self-justification?" Helen asked.

"Maybe, I don't know. What I do know is that he has a genuine interest in the tactics and theory of warfare. I think in the Victor incident, he knew that one of the boys was bound to try it on. He also knew that it would probably be the top dog and dealing to him savagely would earn him both respect and acceptance, even from Victor once he realized that Hamish wasn't interested in knocking him off his perch. Hamish told me that Charles Upham dealt to an army bully in a similar way. Do you know the boys call him Killer? They seem to like him in a weird sort of way. Not that he cares. In fact, he utterly ignores them most of the time."

"Hmm. I think I'll get him to write a detailed account of what he thinks happened that night. Might turn something up."

Helen looked back to Hamish's journal. "What's with this word game you two play?" she asked Terry.

"Dunno really. Just happened. As you know, in any first encounter a bit of shadow boxing goes on. I was pandering to his intellectual vanity, I suppose, trying to find a way in. In Hamish's mind, big words equate with intelligence. I figured that if I treated him as an adult and threw in the odd big word, he might take the bait. Worked like a charm. He also hates talking about himself. He actually told me he's been counseled to death. So for our first couple of sessions we just yakked—about history mostly. I tell you, if he ever went on a TV quiz show, he would clean up totally on Alexander the Great. Did you know that Alexander ended up controlling an empire of over two million square miles and that—"

"Yes, yes," Helen interrupted, "he wrote me five bloody pages about Alexander and even after I asked him not to write any more, he follows it up with another bloody boring piece on Alexander's childhood—thankfully a good bit shorter! Yes, all very interesting, but the fact remains that your little brain box is extremely violent. It's just pure luck the fork missed Victor's eye. I want his next journal entry to be on his perceptions of why he does these things. And tell him that he is welcome to write all he wants about his warrior mates, but not in his journal writing."

## Journal Entry 2—May 20

The first thing I have to do in this entry is to write my version of what happened the day I arrived here. How utterly boring, considering I have already done this. Okay, then, this will be a black-and-white, factual report. I will call myself "the subject" to show you all that I am writing from a totally non-biased point of view. For those of you who don't know, this is called writing objectively!

1500 hours: Subject, Hamish Lance Graham, arrives at New Horizons Boys' Home accompanied by Mr. M. Lewis, a social worker from Warburton Boys' Home. Subject is taken directly to meet Principal and Deputy Principal Mrs. H. Grenville and Mr. S. Whittle. Before departing, Lewis recommends a very careful integration into the school, but New Horizons' managers appear to be unintelligent and are not willing to listen to this sound advice. They say that they will ensure that no harm comes to the subject when he meets the other boys. Lewis is seen to smirk before leaving. Subject endures a long and extremely tedious interview. Subject answers all questions directly, although he is aware that they have all the answers in the files on the desk in front of them and are simply going through an amateurish attempt to become better acquainted with the thinking patterns of the subject. Subject forms seriously negative impression of the intellectual caliber of the staff.

1600 hours: Subject taken to another interview room, where he is introduced to his new social worker, Mr. Terry Swanson, whose numerous tattoos and body piercings do not inspire confidence in the subject. Fortunately this appears to be a rash judgment, because Terry proves to have an extensive vocabulary and has no desire to treat the subject like some sort of weird freak. He also knows a bit more about Alexander the Great than the average punter, although his knowledge of Te Rauparaha and Charles Upham leaves a lot to be desired. Subject makes mental note to rectify this situation.

1645 hours: Subject taken to dormitory, where he stores his clothes, books and general stationery equipment. Terry collects him and gives him a tour of the facility. This gives subject the opportunity to interrogate Terry about the other boys in the institution, particularly about who is the top dog and where his first encounter with the boys will be. Terry takes all this to be nerves on subject's part. Subject cleverly gains detailed information about the combat zone, the number of combatants, the weapons at hand, the number of supervising staff and other necessary reconnaissance information for a successful initial foray into enemy territory.

1730 hours: Subject is brought into dining room for the evening meal and for his initial contact with the other boys. Subject rapidly senses that most of the boys are quite hostile, despite giving the outward appearance, for the staff's sake, of nonchalance. Subject also senses that he is not perceived as any sort of physical threat and is reassured by this mistake. Subject knows that the initial assault will happen at some stage during this meal, mainly because the other boys are all staring at him the same way a starving lion stares at a baby zebra. Subject is seated opposite a tough-looking, muscular boy of about fifteen called Victor Kaiarahi, who, as Terry has described, is definitely the top of the pecking order. Subject notes that several of the boys are trying hard to copy Victor's dress and hairstyle and are even imitating his walking mannerisms. Subject is also aware that the boys are eagerly looking forward to their first strike against the newcomer.

1745 hours: The strike comes sooner than subject expects and in the form of Victor knocking the entire contents of a large glass of milk into subject's meal and all over his shirt and trousers. This is a clever initial strike as it is designed to cause maximum humiliation to subject, under the totally plausible cover of it being an "accident." Subject delays reaction for three seconds while Victor turns to receive the laughs and accolades of his troops, then subject selects a large, four-pronged fork and, standing and stabbing in one motion, drives the fork deep into the soft tissue under Victor's left cheekbone. The fork hits bone and remains embedded for several seconds but is flung out when subject launches his secondary attack before Victor's troops or the staff have a chance to intervene. Subject hits Victor hard in the nose with the heel of his hand and both crash to the floor, closely followed by several other boys and a couple of staff members. Considerable damage is done to dining room furniture in next two minutes, particularly from a considerably overweight boy called Raymond Maihi, who appears to be enjoying himself immensely. Subject is impressed by the authority and strength of a staff member called Mr. Wihongi who singlehandedly stops the fight and then takes Victor away for medical treatment.

1800 hours: Subject is removed from the dining room and placed under close supervision for remainder of night. Subject is pleased at outcome of initial encounter and is confident that he has the respect of his fellow inmates. He is aware, of course, of the need to square things up with Victor once he returns from hospital. Victor will be assured that subject has no desire to topple him from his top dog perch.

End of Report

Now Mrs. Grenville wants me to write about why I am in this place. As I said before, this is much better than talking about it because I don't have to waste time explaining obvious bits to the counselors, who, apart from Terry, are actually pretty thick.

It is obvious why I am here. I am in here because sometimes I do very violent things and I am too young to be put in jail, although I have been in two "secure youth facilities"—well, three if you count this one, but you could hardly call it secure. A retarded gorilla could dismantle the alarms. I can walk out anytime I want!

I think I have always been violent, but I decided to start doing hardout violent things when I was about eight. I might stop being violent one day because life is all about choices. My first major violent act was when I was in Year 4 at school. I went there on a Sunday morning, climbed in a window and smashed up all the science fair projects in the hall. I just felt like it. I also went into some classrooms and did stuff like kill all the turtles and frogs in an aquarium and kill two budgies by squeezing them so hard that they died. I could feel their little bones breaking. When I told the principal that it was me, and not teenage boys like other people had said, she didn't believe me at first. I had to explain to her exactly how I had climbed in the window before she believed me. She looked at me for quite a while and then began yelling.

The next major violent thing I did happened when I was about ten, and unless you were on Mars when this happened, you will know about it. I pushed an old man off a wharf and he hit his head on the way down and drowned. It was at the Miramar wharf in Wellington, and the old man was from Iraq. He was fishing with some other old Iraqi men and for at least an hour they were talking loudly, in their own language. I was into fishing big-time at this stage and usually tried to fish near quiet people. But I am very tolerant of other cultures and usually like hearing different languages, so I didn't mind their jabbering so much, even if it was a weird language with lots of high annoying bits that hurt my ears and lots of noises that sounded like spitting. But then they started arguing really loudly, apparently over some missing fish bait. I tried to tell them that I saw a seagull take off with it and that if they spent less time talking and more time concentrating on fishing, they wouldn't have lost it. I even offered them some of my salted squid bait to shut them up, but they ignored me totally. It was like I didn't even exist. They just argued louder and louder. This made me really angry because it was a stupid thing for adults to argue over and I got that sort of intense white noise you get in your head when your ears hurt, so I stood up and yelled at them to "shut the fuck up!" They were shocked and just stared at me and then they began to point and laugh. They laughed for ages, hitting their knees and carrying on, and the noise began to hurt my ears again so I ran hard at the man doing most of the laughing and pushed him over the edge of the wharf into the water.

It was my fault that he fell into the water, because I pushed him, but it was not my fault that he hit his head on the way down, because I didn't know that there was a big beam sticking out. He should have just swum back to the ladder that was there, but his head was sort of split open at the back and all this gunk came out. He just floundered about for a bit and then sank. I don't want to write more about this because it will get boring. It was in all the papers and on TV for ages and even on talk radio, where people said I should be flogged and stuff like that. The courts didn't really know what to do with me because I was too young to be put into a secure youth facility. The family court judge actually asked me what I thought should happen to me. I told him that executing me would be a reasonable punishment, or if they didn't want to do that, then they should cut off one of my hands, because this used to be a fairly common punishment in Iraq. He thought I was being a smart-ass and got quite angry with me. I then said that if they were too chicken to execute or mutilate me, I should be flogged to within an inch of my life. He thought I was just being smart again, but I said that I had heard a man saying this about me on talk radio and the announcer and most of the other callers seemed to think that it was a damn good idea, so why the hell was he freaking out at me for suggesting it? I even told the judge that the Iraqi guy's family should do the flogging, you know, share it around. I explained to him that this would make them all feel a lot better and that it would be good justice. Everyone in the courtroom began looking at me very weirdly after I said that.

*Flog* is a very cool word. If you say it slowly, you can almost feel the pain. Go on, try it! See? Told you! There was this prisoner on Norfolk Island who was flogged to death. He really annoyed the authority guys, so he was sentenced to 250 lashes of the cat-o'-nine-tails. He died of blood loss and shock after about 200 lashes, but they had to keep flogging him because the governor said he had to get 250 lashes, so 250 is what he got. Flogging a dead man. Now that's violent! I sometimes imagine myself as that man being flogged and then I imagine myself as the man wielding the cat-o'-nine-tails. The weird thing is that the man doing the flogging was another prisoner who had greased his way into the job. He was found with his throat cut the day after the flogging. Good job!

The Bible reckons that Jesus was flogged big-time before he was crucified, but he can't have been flogged that hard because he still had the strength to carry his cross up a hill. Mind you, he was still a really tough guy and didn't make a big fuss when the Roman soldiers made him wear this hardout crown of thorns and hammered nails through his wrists and feet.

I have considered letting Jesus join my team (Alexander the Great, Charles Upham and Te Rauparaha) because by all accounts he was an excellent

43

leader, but he was mostly into the peace and love scene and I doubt he would approve of stuff like mass slaughter, even if it was really justified. Anyway, it's pretty hard to work out what actually took place with Jesus because religion makes people a bit crazy and want to believe silly stuff, like Jesus being able to change water into wine and being able to raise the dead—yeah right! Mind you, I can relate to the bravery of some of the early Christian martyrs. I went to a Sunday school for a while (until the idiot running it told my mother not to bring me back for some reason—real Christian attitude—not!) and a lady gave us this cool book about how some early Christians were burned and mutilated for their faith. There was this one mad picture where these guys were being slowly roasted alive over a sort of brazier. In the end I was told to stop asking questions about it and my book was taken off me! I reckon we know heaps more about Alexander the Great than Jesus, even though Alexander lived 370 years before him.

As I said before, you will probably know all about me pushing the old man in the water, unless you were overseas (or on Mars) at the time. If you were, you can just go to a library or something and get back copies of newspapers for July 2002. But if you do that, don't believe it when the papers said I laughed as he hit his head and drowned. I didn't laugh when he drowned because that would have been a stupid thing to do in the circumstances. I did, however, think that it was quite funny that heaps of small fish were attracted to all the blood and the little bits of flesh that were floating in the water. Even though I was young, I was able to appreciate the irony of the men arguing about fish bait and then the main guy doing the arguing being turned into fish bait! But I was not laughing at the man drowning. The papers made a mistake there and no one would let me explain. And anyway, I was only ten.

# 101
# CHAPTER THREE

"So what's he like to work with? I mean, he sounds to me like a pretentious little prat." Sarah Quinn handed Terry her copy of Hamish's latest journal entry. She had highlighted several sections. "I mean, look at this bit here: 'I might stop being violent one day because life is all about choices.' What's that about?"

"I tell you, he is a thinker. He's probably repeating what various counselors have drummed into him over the years, but he does have a remarkable ability to analyze himself. I really look forward to our sessions. He is so different to most of the cowboys here." Terry was about to continue, but Helen popped a head into his office.

"Heard that last bit and have to disagree. What we

have here is life according to Hamish. He is leaving out crucial information because it makes him look bad. He is articulate, persuasive and, I suspect, extremely manipulative, but I wonder if he's so very different to a lot of boys his age? I know for a fact that he smashed up the school because of hurt pride over a rejected science fair project, and I have spoken to Milly Polachoric about the assault. His version is wishful thinking to say the least."

Terry swung back in his chair. "I'm not saying that his versions of events are accurate, but I still think he shows uncanny insight into how he operates. He interests me."

"Terry, I put him on your caseload because of your experience with, um, let's say 'unusual' boys, but take it carefully. I don't want a Hamish fan club starting up here. I'm going to tell him to rewrite the school vandalism episode and the assault on Milly again. I'm figuring he'll tell the truth this time. Let's see what you think of him then."

## Journal Entry 3—June 1

Mrs. Grenville says that this journal writing will not work if I am not honest and leave important bits out. She reckons I'm glossing over the truth. She wasn't interested in getting into an argument about what truth means. I asked, "Whose truth—yours or mine?" She reckoned I was avoiding the issue by playing with words. I don't think she understands that there is no such thing as a neutral "truth" because everything humans do is clouded with emotion. Last year I read this very cool old book called *Nineteen Eighty-Four,* by George Orwell. In the book, Britain is ruled by this hardcore party who brainwash the people into accepting as truth and reality whatever the party says is truth and reality. If they say $2 + 2 = 5$, then that is what it is and to think otherwise is treason. The best part in the book was when the authorities tortured the main character, Winston Smith, by exposing him to his greatest fear. In his case it was rats, and his head was enclosed in this rat cage and giant rats were let loose on him. Not quite sure what my greatest fear would be. Nothing as lame as rats or giant spiders, that's for sure. Maybe if they locked me in a small room full of particularly stupid people—no, I've got it. To be stuck in a broken elevator with a bunch of ultra-moronic people would totally freak me out. This Orwell guy was like a major pessimist and thought the world he lived in was heading in the same direction as the world in his book, I suppose. You can see his point, though. Think about all the brainwashing we get through the media and all the other ways we are under

surveillance these days. I'm not going to get into this—
way over the heads of most people around here.

Well, no big deal, I'll tell you the "truth." Doesn't
worry me! She accepted that the drowning stuff was all
true but reckoned I was not being honest about the
hippie counselor or smashing up the science exhibits.
I have to write about those two things again. So don't
blame me if you get totally bored and want to throw this
journal away or rip out every single page or even burn
it! I would.

I will tell you about the science fair fiasco first. (Terry
will like reading that last bit because another game we
have is creating whole chunks of alliteration.) Anyway,
what happened was, I was very proud of my science fair
project, which, oddly enough, was on rats and how they
deal with problems. Mum bought me four rats and Dad
made a cool cage with separate compartments for them.
I kept the cage in the garage under a sheet and I made
it quite clear that no one was allowed to look except me.
I had read somewhere that if the world was hit by a
nuclear holocaust, rats would be the most likely
mammal to survive. This makes them really hard-core
survivors, so my idea was to find out how strong their
survival instinct actually is. One simple, practical way of
testing this would be to find out what sort of things I

would have to do to make them stop eating their favorite food, which for my rats was little bits of cooked bacon. Anything wrong with any of this so far? Exactly! At first I just put different obstacles in their way and timed them on working out how to get to the bacon. This was okay, but nothing out of the ordinary. I knew that the judges would be bored with that and think that I was stupid or worse, say, "Well done," and give me a certificate of merit or some such condescending crap. So I decided to handicap the rats in different, interesting ways. With one rat I tied quite a heavy lead fishing sinker around his stomach. I had to use wire because he kept biting through the fishing nylon and string I tried first. He could still move, but it took him ages and the wire was cutting into his body. The weird thing was that he continued to drag himself to the food, but he kept getting thinner during the week leading up to the fair. The second rat had it easy because I just tied his back legs together with wire. He got around easily and was funny to watch. That one ate heaps and got quite fat. The last rat had the hardest job because I cut one of his legs off with Dad's fishing knife. He moved in circles a lot and ate stuff-all after that, but maybe that was because of the infection that set in around the wound. It was quite tricky stopping the blood flow and in the end I had to cauterize the stump with a red-hot knife. This one ended up smelling quite bad as well. As I said, there was a fourth rat, but that one died when I was working out how to do things to them without them freaking out and biting me. I ended up making them cool little funnel collars from drink cans. I mean, that alone should have won me first prize in the competition.

I am quite aware that some people reading this will be thinking all this sounds cruel, but it wasn't because it was for a scientific experiment. If I was just doing it for a laugh, it would be cruel, but I wasn't, so it couldn't have been. I also made up a big display board with diagrams, flowcharts, timelines and bar graphs explaining everything I had done. I put a lot of work into it and was feeling quite proud.

Dad dropped me off at school that morning and carried the cage in for me. No one was allowed to look under the sheet because it was going to be a big surprise. When Dad put it down on my desk, I got one of the boys to do a pretend drumroll and then I whipped off the sheet like a magician and all the kids came to look. Two stupid girls began to scream when they saw my rats, although some of the boys thought it was cool the way the rat with the missing leg was chewing at the stump and that the rat with the weight tied to it was making a tiny, high noise and bleeding a lot. My teacher got very upset and fetched the principal, who freaked out big-time. I tried to tell her that I got the idea from the Internet and that vivisection using rats is very popular with heaps of intelligent scientists and that the makeup she was wearing too much of had probably been force-fed to rats during testing. She began to yell at me, and at Dad too, and made him take me and the rats home.

Heaps of dumb parents complained that their kids were traumatized by my experiment. Their kids are far more likely to be traumatized from being brought up by retarded parents than by seeing my science project. I was even suspended from school for three days when I gave the girl doing most of the complaining a little push. What an overreaction! So that's why I got angry with the school and smashed up the science fair exhibits. Mine was easily the best, but the teachers thought it was stupid and cruel. They awarded the first prize to a really lame project about how fast wheat can sprout under different conditions. Yawn! No one listened to me when I said that her experiment was a lame version of mine—she used wheat and I used rats. Who are we to say that the wheat grains lying in the dried-up soil weren't being abused, like my rats supposedly were? Wheat is a living thing—a rat is a living thing. The rats may have been fine about sacrificing their lives for a greater cause anyway. Did anyone ask them? The girl who made that project was brain-dead dumb and her parents must have done all the work—if you can call growing wheat in ice-cream containers work. The only prize her wheat experiment should have won was in an insomnia-curing competition. I made sure I smashed up that one good and proper. I think I may have pissed on it too, but I can't remember.

And now for the hippie counselor bit. You are probably ultra-bored by now, and like I said before, you are very welcome to rip out this page or burn it or something. I probably would if I had to read it shortly after having already read a perfectly acceptable version of the events.

Anyway, the counselor was going on and on about my childhood and how I needed to let go of stuff. Usually when people do this sort of talking to me, I make up a game where I pretend that they are talking a different language and I can't understand it. It's easy to do and soon the words do begin to sound really strange. I used to do this at school a lot to pass the time. I also used to invent my own languages and once spoke an invented language for several weeks. I got to the stage of writing out a basic vocabulary list of almost 300 words, which I distributed to the people in my class and said they all had to learn. Most of the kids were pretty useless at remembering the vocab, but heaps of them learned the various swearwords and used them for ages. I got stuck when I was trying to work out basic verbs—how to change them to show past, present and future tenses. If you didn't count all the kids using the new swearwords, I reckon I had at least thirty kids in the school speaking bits of my language, although not many latched onto my idea of changing a meaning from positive to negative by using changes in tone and volume instead of using prefixes. For example, to make the negative of the word *lucky,* we use the prefix *un* to get the new word *unlucky.* In my language, the word for *lucky* was *vot* and to show the opposite meaning you had to stretch the *o* sound and give it a rise in tone.

But once again the dim-witted principal complained to my parents. Maybe her job description read "must have limited intellect and the inability to challenge bright students." She called my language "subversive" and said it undermined staff authority. Yeah right! You've got to *have* authority before it can be undermined.

I only agreed to stop when I came to the conclusion that it is virtually impossible to fast-track a new language. Language has to evolve over a long period because it kind of reflects a culture and all the ingredients that have gone into making it. I think that must be why that made-up language called Esperanto never took off big-time. A Polish guy called Dr. Zamenhof made it up in 1877 and he must have been super-bright because it is like a whole, real language with very cool verb forms. But like I said, it didn't really reflect a cultural group of people, just one guy's attempt at world peace through having a common European language. He gave it a good shot, though, and I can't work out why he isn't an international hero. Bet none of you have ever heard of him!

Anyway, back to the counselor. I got bored with this game and decided to try her out on the "staring at the chest" game. This is another one that usually works well and from my experience can really unsettle bossy ladies. Not that I am a sex pervert or anything, but it is a very good tactic. If you don't believe me, try it sometime. She was a bit of a tough cookie this one, though, and when she realized what I was doing, she didn't get pissed off or anything, so I stared harder. Then she started laughing hardout and said, "What's up, honey? Didn't you get enough titty when you were a baby?" I'm not quite sure why, but this made me lose it big-time and I think I pushed her over and punched her a few times or maybe I hit her with something sharp. I can't recall what I did really, but she ran out of the room screaming with blood coming from between her fingers.

It annoys me that I can't recall all the things that I do when I get really angry. It's not the anger but the loss of control that worries me because I like to be in control at all times. That's why I don't use alcohol or try drugs. Well, I did try alcohol once. I pinched a bottle of whiskey from Dad's booze cabinet and drank about half before I chucked up everywhere. I felt as sick as a dog and could barely talk. Yeah, I looked real clever. Stuff that! I don't know if other people have this feeling, but when I get really angry, I get this kind of intense white-colored noise in my head. I know noises don't have colors, but this noise does. It's like a vibrating or grating noise behind my eyes, with a red or sometimes white feel to it. I have told several counselors about this over the years and they go on about giving me ways of controlling and diluting my anger. This is pointless because I don't want to dilute my anger. What I want is to be more in control when I get angry so I can remember it all and analyze the body response more. I would love to be able to channel the physical strength I sometimes have when I get color-noise angry. Even though I'm a bit skinny, I am actually quite strong and can perform amazing feats of strength when I'm color-noise angry. There was this one time when I was about eleven or twelve and I smashed my bedroom door right off its hinges. The builder who came to fix it didn't believe that I could have done it. We lived in an old villa and the *kauri* door weighed about a ton. You don't want to fight me when I'm color-noise angry either—no way! So anyway, you can see that there were some things in my first version of events that were true.

After I attacked the counselor, two orderlies took me to isolation, which is actually pretty cool because I didn't have to talk to anyone stupid. For two days I thought about Alexander the Great, Charles Upham and Te Rauparaha, imagining how cool it would have been if they were all in the same army, and I was with them. I also invented a very interesting board game about them, which is a sort of mixture of the games Snakes and Ladders and Trivial Pursuit and a book called *The Dice Man.* I called my game Go for Your Life!

*The Dice Man* is this very cool old book about a guy who decides to allow a toss of the dice to rule the decisions he has to make in life. It works like this: for every decision you have to make, like "What will I do on the weekend?" you write down six possibilities. Four have to be fairly reasonable things, like go to the movies or walk the dog or whatever; one has to be a real treat, like buy a new phone or eat a whole pavlova; and one has to be ultra-dangerous or undesirable, like telling the toughest kid in the school he's a fat wanker or pinching the deputy principal's bum. Of course, in the book it ends up getting the guy into all sorts of trouble and he kills himself.

I decided to play the dice game for a while after I read the book when I was twelve, but Mum made me stop when I began getting into all sorts of trouble. Mind you, I did make the game more exciting by having two bad options every time. The last two times I played it were very intense. On the second-to-last time (penultimate time, eh, Terry?) I made one of the options killing a wild beast, and sure enough it came up and I had to do it. But as we have a shortage of wild beasts in this country, I thought that killing a gang member's dog would be a good substitute. Here's what happened.

Once when Dad got lost in Upper Hutt we passed the headquarters of a gang who called themselves Satans Slaves and I recall being quite surprised and also pleased that people would want to build a kind of military fortress in the middle of a suburb. I figured that they probably had heaps of mean pit bull terrier sort of dogs running loose and decided that breaking into their fortress and killing one of their wild beasts was a worthy challenge. I was feeling pretty nervous on the train out to Upper Hutt, but I comforted myself by thinking about how brave eleven-year-old Alexander was when, armed only with a short stabbing sword, he killed a charging wild boar. The nearest thing I could find to a short sword was one of Mum's carving knives, so I sharpened that up and put it in my bag.

When I finally found the house, I had to figure out how to get in because there was a high wall right around the place. I decided to wait until someone was either coming in or going out, and sure enough, a couple of minutes later two men pulled up on motorbikes and spoke into a very cool intercom contraption beside the gate. The gate then seemed to open automatically and I slipped in after the bikes and hid behind an old car. Things didn't go according to plan after that, though, because the only dog they seemed to own was an elderly Labrador that somehow sniffed me out and sat before me with its tail wagging. I decided to try and make it angry so that it would try to attack me and then I could stab it with my knife, but when I gave it a bit of a kick and chased it with the knife, it ran away howling. This is when I was caught by one of the gang members.

He knocked the knife out of my hand and dragged me inside to the boss Satans Slaves guy. They were all pretty stunned that a thirteen-year-old kid had sneaked into the property and for some reason was trying to kill their elderly pet dog with a carving knife.

Their leader was a tattooed, wiry man called Neil and he seemed quite impressed when I said that I was doing it because a roll of the dice said I had to kill a wild beast. To cut a long story short, he made me a mug of Milo and began to tell me about the Satans Slaves and what they stood for. One of Neil's heroes turned out to be Adolf Hitler, but he hadn't even read *Mein Kampf,* so I filled him in on a few details. He wasn't all that pleased when I told him that in my opinion Hitler was a stupid choice for a hero because he was such a poor military strategist. I told him that if he was determined to have a World War Two German hero, then he should have the leader of the Afrika Korps, General Erwin Rommel, because he was their finest strategist and a very brave soldier.

I also couldn't help but point out to Neil and the others that the name "Satans Slaves" was actually fairly lame and that if they wanted to be taken seriously, then a better name would be something like Rommel's Raiders. I even drew them a new patch design for their jackets. It was a very cool picture of a tank emerging from a storm cloud, all guns blazing and superimposed over a large grinning skull with blood dripping from the eye sockets. Neil got all excited about this and suggested I start up a youth division of his gang and that I could be the leader. An immediate task for me would be to deal with the little gangsters who kept tagging their fence. He figured that if I was staunch enough to break into their headquarters to try to kill their dog, then I could easily deal with a bunch of junior hoods. I said I would give his proposition serious thought. Neil wouldn't hear of me catching the train home and gave me a lift on his Harley motorbike. Mum got a major surprise when Neil roared up the driveway and dropped me off.

The final roll of the dice challenge didn't have quite such a happy ending. I got beaten up quite badly because I had to push this huge Samoan boy down the stairs at my school. He wasn't hurt much because he sort of bounced down the stairs, but he made a really big fuss about it and he and his two mates gave me the bash big-time. They didn't want to hear about why I had to do it and showed much less tolerance than Neil and his mates.

Anyway, as I said, my game is a combination of

Snakes and Ladders, Trivial Pursuit and *The Dice Man,* although I reckon mine is much better because you don't ever get bored in my game. (Unless you're stupid, but I'll have big warnings on the box saying: WARNING— NOT FOR STUPID PEOPLE! I could have a sort of basic IQ test on the outside of the box so stupid people, most of whom are tragically unaware of how stupid they actually are, don't waste their money.) It takes several days to play it properly because if you land in certain squares, you have to read up on the heroic deeds from my three main men and then try to imitate their deeds in a variety of simulated situations. All good things. You can also land in bad news squares on the board and have to suffer the consequences. This part of the game will require more thought because I doubt that I will be allowed to sell a game where you have to seriously hurt people or destroy property. Anyway, I expect to make a lot of money out of this game, so I'm not going to tell you any more about it in case anyone reading this rips off my ideas. When I was finally let out of isolation, I was told I had to come to this new place.

# 101
## CHAPTER FOUR

Wearing a tight little smile, Simon Whittle sauntered into Helen's cramped office and tossed a copy of Hamish's latest journal onto her desk. "Mystery solved. The boy's barking mad. In my opinion he suffers from classic delusions of grandeur mixed with some sort of pathological phobia of being thought stupid. We aren't the place for him. We deal with bad kids, not mad kids."

Helen had been expecting this confrontation for several days now and remained calm.

"Ah, yes, Simon, because there is such a clear division between madness and badness, isn't there? I mean, our prisons are full of totally sane bad people, right? Have you thought about Hamish's auditory intolerance? I don't know about you, but I find that quite fascinating. I was just talking to Terry about some wonderful research coming out of Scandinavia suggesting—"

"What the . . . ? Listen to yourself. We just don't have the time or resources to delve into that, however fascinating you and Terry find it to be. We have four new placements next week. Let's move this oddball on to those who have the time to deal with him and get on with the core business of this place. Hamish has to go!"

"And is that your considered professional opinion, Simon? Have you spoken to him, even once? It sounds like you're already preparing a case for permanent incarceration in a psych unit."

"Helen, we have twenty-five high-maintenance boys in this place and no shortage of future clients, yet you and Terry seem to spend most of the day obsessing over one spoiled, middle-class, delusional brat. The boy has serious mental health issues. And yes, it is my professional opinion, and no, I haven't spoken to him. Look, Helen, this really isn't the place for a boy like Hamish. He appears to be utterly unpredictable and I think he needs help in a more secure environment. He is definitely dangerous to himself and others."

"What are you suggesting? A hospital for the criminally insane, like some sort of junior Hannibal Lecter?"

"You've studied Hamish for over a month now. Admit it, Helen—we aren't set up for cases like him. He has killed once, viciously assaulted a therapist, and could easily have done serious damage to Victor Kaiarahi on his first bloody day here. What next? We have to make sure we aren't being seduced by his intelligence and allowing ourselves to be manipulated. Face it, he has to go, and soon. And don't start going about the so-called calming effect he has on the boys. He's just as likely to cut their throats!"

"But he does calm them down—you must have noticed that. When he's with them, there seems to be less hassling and fewer squabbles. Victor is still the boss, but the boys really look up to Hamish and want him to like them. And you have to agree that he is having a positive effect on Noel Mackintosh."

"Oh bullshit! Noel spends all day shadowing him. God knows what bizarre behavior he's picking up. No, Hamish has to go and you know it."

**Journal Entry 4—June 20**

Now I have to write about my fellow inmates (Mrs. Grenville doesn't like that word and tries to say we are clients—what a load of crap!). Here goes. This will be a short journal entry because, with the exception of Victor and Noel, the other boys are all extremely boring people.

I have discovered that Victor is very intelligent. This will no doubt be a big surprise to all you wise people running this place (apart from Mr. Wihongi) because you treat him like the dumb thug he pretends to be. The first couple of days after I attacked him were a bit tense and I could tell he was aching for a chance to crack my head open, so I approached him and said I wanted to sort things out between us. He was pleased and thought this meant a scrap, but I said that we needed to work out a treaty plan. He was suspicious at first, but when I pointed out that we were like two superpowers operating in the same disputed territory, he knew straightaway what I was talking about. I said that as he was bigger and stronger than me, he was quite capable of giving me a hiding anytime he wanted to, but I also pointed out that I was unlike most other opponents because I had absolutely no fear of him and that I would use whatever weapons I could lay my hands on in a scrap. He knew this already! We decided that he was still the boss, but that no one was to hassle me in any way at all and that he and the others were to stop hassling a new kid, Noel, who had joined us. Victor agreed to all this, so we shook on it and then had a bit of a yarn about how he ended up here. So here's the stuff you should know about Victor but probably don't.

Victor is Maori, and he is originally from a little town on the East Coast called Tolaga Bay. He is the youngest of seven children, and although there was never much money at his home, life was pretty sweet when he was a kid. When money was scarce, he and various brothers and uncles would head inland to hunting huts and stock up on venison and wild pork. Victor excelled at bushcraft and stuck his first wild pig when he was only eleven—the same as you know who! His uncle Sid was pretty pissed off at first because it was a mean old tusker that had killed at least two of his dogs the last time they had it bailed up and he'd wanted to kill the beast himself, but Victor was fitter and got there first. Lucky he did because one dog was already down and the others were losing ground fast. Victor didn't pause to think of the danger, just leapt in and thrust his hunting knife deep into the old boar's throat. Man, I would have loved to have seen that!

Victor said that in primary school, he was always top of the class and all his *whanau* had high hopes for him. He continued to do well at high school, but this is where his academic ability first began to be a burden. He was a naturally popular boy and had the physique and sporting ability to earn the ongoing respect of his peers. But from Year 9 on it was as if a mysterious wall had come between them. At the end of his first year of high school, when he received a whole heap of awards at prizegiving, Victor was aware that the applause had a sort of distant, respectful quality to it and, without understanding why, he knew that this was going to be a problem. Things were changing in his secure little world and he felt on edge a lot of the time. The teachers didn't help by continually referring to his leadership qualities and the *mana* he would surely bring to his school when he went on to do well at university. He especially hated it when they sucked up to him by automatically putting him in charge if they were doing some sort of group activity or always asking him to give the *karakia* if they were having *kai*.

Victor hated the way his mates' parents began to treat him differently too, always making sure he got the biggest kai portions and sugar already stirred into his tea, an honor usually reserved for the elderly. He didn't want to be a leader, he just wanted to be Victor and have fun with his mates. To make up for this, he tried to be a badass and would pick fights or challenge his mates in outrageous stunts of bravado, like seeing how long they could stand on the back of a galloping horse before being thrown. Again, allowances were made and he got away with stuff that any other local kid would have been cut down for big-time. So Victor decided that the only way to totally blend in with the other kids was to stop being so predictably successful at everything. He rebelled. He started to skip class and hang out with an older bunch of boys, most of whom no longer attended school and spent their days drinking, smoking dope and getting up to mischief. He even developed his own tag: a *V* with a little crown over it. He refused to go hunting with his uncles, claiming it was boring. His family and the teachers at school were devastated, of course, but seemed powerless to bring him to his senses.

Help came from an unlikely source, his brother Charlie, the acknowledged black sheep of the family. Charlie, the hard case who seemed to have been in trouble since he could walk. Charlie, who had left home at fourteen, became a patched gang member at seventeen and now, at the ripe old age of nineteen, was a Hastings-based gang enforcer with a fearsome physique that backed up his growing reputation. But when he heard from one of his sisters that little Victor was going off the rails, he immediately came home and tried to talk some sense into him. Charlie quietly visited each of Victor's new mates and let them know that if they wished to see another sunrise, they would leave him alone. This subtle persuasion had the desired effect and the two brothers became close for the first time. Charlie told Victor that, like it or not, he was special and that he had a responsibility to do his best and not end up following in his footsteps. He had to hook up again with his real mates. Charlie formed a serious pact with his brother. If Victor returned to school full time, Charlie said he would drop the patch, leave the gang and join the army—something he had been toying with for a while but never had the guts or motivation to put into action. This lifted a lot of pressure off Victor because for a while Charlie became the center of attention. Before he left for his army training in Waiouru, he was even asked to speak at a school assembly as an example of a young man who had the courage to turn his back on gangs and take a positive step forward in his life. So Victor returned to school and all was well for a while.

The "mates" of Victor who Charlie put the frighteners up had the last roll of the dice, though. One night after Charlie had left, they persuaded Victor to come for one final joyride with them. At some stage in the drunken night they threw a Molotov cocktail through the window of the high school library, burning it to the ground. A neighbor saw their car speeding away from the scene and Victor was charged with being an accessory to a crime. But fate wasn't finished with Victor's family. The numbing shame of this was compounded a few days later by the terrible news that Charlie had died in an army training accident. A great and prolonged sadness engulfed the family.

Victor was eventually sent to live with relatives in West Auckland, where he barely attended school and quickly fell into bad company. He was an angry time bomb and took little time to make his mark. In a matter of weeks he became the kingpin in a group of out-of-it street kids. Things came to a head when Victor badly beat up the leader of an older crew who was supposed to be in charge of the suburb. He got done for causing grievous bodily harm, and as you know, that's how Victor ended up here. He is still torn apart by his brother's death and no doubt blames himself for a lot of the family's problems. Terry told me that, apart from me, the only boy to ever seriously challenge Victor's rule of the place was Raymond, who despite his size advantage, got a total beating.

Despite all this strife he still seems to me to be a genuine leader and a born warrior, but he needs to be understood and mentally and physically challenged. He would have been great in the 28th Maori Battalion in the Second World War; in fact, most of the "bad" Maori kids I have met would thrive in a genuine war situation. It's not true that they can't hack discipline; it's all about who's giving the orders. I have noticed the way Victor reacts when given an order by Mr. Wihongi. There's none of the surliness or posturing you people see. There's something about those two that I'm not quite sure about. Sometimes Mr. Wihongi almost seems to be deliberately picking on Victor, setting higher standards for him than the others, and then at other times he seems to be protecting him from the staff. Like the time when Mr. Whittle blamed Victor for acts of vandalism to a toilet block. Whittle doubted that it really was his fault, but figured that punishing Victor was the best way of finding out who actually did the damage. Even though Whittle outranked him, Mr. Wihongi rescued Victor from solitary and gave Whittle a public barreling about never again shaming Victor in such a way. Mr. Whittle went so red, I thought he would explode. I like mysteries and will keep an eye on this one. I told Victor about officer careers in the army as I reckon he could do really well. He sort of clammed up a bit when I said that, but I suppose it's to do with his brother's death. Anyway, that's enough about Victor. But make sure you add my information to your obviously inadequate files. You're lucky I'm not charging you for doing your job!

Now I'm going to write about Noel. All you lot know is that he got a hard time when he arrived and that it mysteriously stopped overnight. You're still probably congratulating yourselves on how well you have done with him—yeah right! Anyway, as you know, two weeks after I was sent here, a fourteen-year-old boy called Noel arrived. He was sent here because he is some sort of serial arsonist, which makes him interesting from the start. (Well, don't leave confidential files lying around in unlocked offices!) When I was about four or five, I had a real thing about fire. Once I set fire to the neighbors' garage to pay them back for their dogs always snarling at me through the fence, and I can still remember the stunning thrill of watching the flames and smoke climb into the sky. A total power blast for a little kid. I stopped starting fires a couple of years later because it really is a kid's game. I always feel kind of sorry for the sad loser adults who get done for arson.

When he arrived, Noel was utterly silent and had withdrawn into his own little world. Right from the start, you lot were all over him like a rash, desperate to make him talk and engage with you all. You reckoned he was suffering from serious depression and until I intervened (ha ha!), you had him on antidepressants. The only one who wanted to leave him alone was Terry, who said Noel would open up in his own good time. Most of the boys put him through hell in the first few weeks with their initiation crap and they nicknamed him "Dumbo." When are you lot going to do something serious about the initiation stuff that goes on here? Don't pretend you don't know what I'm on about either! They only stopped hassling Noel after Victor told them to leave him alone and said that Noel and I were going to be mates.

And now for the embarrassing part for you geniuses who run this place. When he'd been here for about a week, I asked Noel if he'd read *One Flew Over the Cuckoo's Nest* or seen the movie. He blanked me out, but I knew I had his attention so I told him about it. I said that he was just like Chief Bromden from the book and that I thought being selectively mute was an excellent way of avoiding being mauled to death by all the do-gooders in this place. But I also pointed out that he needed to do something to stop the guys hassling him and that if he wanted to, he could hang around me for a bit because no one hassles me. I got a smile out of him when I said that if he was going to hang around me, he had to be quiet because I had a lot of thinking to do and can't stand noisy kids.

It's not such a mystery why he remains silent. It turns out he has got a wicked stammer and is sick of dealing with it. The staff here (yes, that's you) must have access to his school and medical records, but none of you seem to have considered a serious speech impediment being the reason for his muteness. I read a magazine article about a guy who stammered. He had to invent ways of communicating without stammering. One way was to speak in various accents and another was to sing information. Isn't it interesting that serious stammerers never stammer when they sing? Noel and I have been experimenting and he can now go for ages without stammering if he speaks in this heavy American accent, a sort of cliché New Jersey accent—like Tony from *The Sopranos.* He can do this really well but only when we are alone somewhere. The others still think he is totally mute. The singing doesn't work because he can't sing for crap, but our best discovery has proved to be a real winner for Noel—rapping. I can't stand rapping—far too boring for me, but Noel has the accent and rhythms down pat. What he isn't so good at is the rhymes, and this is where I have been helping him. We think of a topic and see how long we can go rapping back and forth. He's got the rhythms and I've got the rhymes. We haven't broken the news to the others yet because I have a plan to make Noel famous forever in Manukau New Horizons Boys' Home. He is going to be the world's first mute winner of a rapping competition. He didn't want a bar of it at first, but I have persuaded him that it will be a total blast and will earn him major respect from the boys, while being a bit of a slap in the face to you lot.

## Journal Entry 4 (Part 2)—June 26

I was right—it was a blast. Admit it, go on! I know most of you were there, but I'll give you the full run-down anyway. I made a couple of posters advertising the competition and the boys were right into it. I know you lot weren't so sure, but I got Terry to convince you by saying cheesy things like, "It will allow the boys to express themselves and let off steam in a creative and fun way." I even got him to convince you to supply pizzas and Coke for the big night. Sorry, Terry, hope I'm not dropping you in it too much.

Victor was the MC for the event, as well as being a one-man sound box for each rapper. He announced the rules for the one-on-one competition. In the first round each rapper was to have one minute to bum the other out. The crowd noise was to decide the winner of each bout, with Victor having the final say if it was a close call. I told Noel he would sit out this round to make his eventual victory all the more unexpected, and I would ensure they let him into the final round as a "wild card entry." When I told them they had to let Noel into the final, they presumed I just wanted to make him look like a real dick in front of everyone and thought it was a great idea, although Victor was a bit taken aback: "That's kind of mean, bro!"

The first round went off well, and I have to admit, the standard was pretty high. It really surprised me that some of the boys who usually conversed in single-syllable grunts were capable of quite complex vocabulary in a rap context. The staff got into it and were laughing and clapping along, especially when some of the guys were doing impromptu krumping between rounds. When it was time for the final, it was obvious that Raymond was the man to beat. The time was increased to two minutes, and after he knocked out each finalist, he sort of did this wild Tarzan roar and beat his big chest. When Noel stepped forward to compete against him, the boys all cracked up big time. Raymond was pissed off at first because, while he enjoyed making fun of Noel, he thought that this was all a bit below a rapper of his instant fame. You lot were also annoyed and tried to intervene. You all thought, of course, that I was playing a vicious joke on Noel, assuming that he had no idea what was going on. You only let it continue when he made it clear by his body language that he wanted to be up there.

Raymond led off with rapid-fire lines mocking Noel, his muteness, his mother, me, my mother, white boys in general and a few good ones about the staff as well. The boys were ecstatic, high-fiving all over the place, and big Raymond was already doing a victory dance. Everyone still thought it was a joke when Noel stepped forward. He just stood there looking away into the distance. Eventually he began to move rhythmically from side to side and do some hand gestures, but then he sort of seized up and stopped. The boys began to laugh, and I thought that maybe the occasion was too much and that I had screwed up big-time. Noel saw that I was just about to go up and rescue him, but he held up a hand and let rip with a rapid-fire diatribe about Raymond, bullies like him, social workers, schools, parents—you name it, he had a crack at it in his two minutes of fame. When he finished, you could hear a pin drop; then the boys erupted, shouting and hooting for all they were worth. Noel was an instant hero and even Raymond eventually joined in the fun, hoisting him onto his broad shoulders and parading him around as the undisputed winner.

# 101

# CHAPTER FIVE

"But I don't see what you are so worked up about. Hamish proved to everyone that there is no psychological reason why Noel Mackintosh isn't speaking and at the same time brilliantly ensured the boys treat him with respect from now on. What is the problem?"

Simon's face was flushed with anger.

"The problem, Terry, is bloody obvious. This whole thing is all about Hamish—all about him proving again what a bunch of idiots we are and what a clever little chappy he is . . ."

"Well, if the cap fits, Simon."

"Oh, grow up! You know what I mean. He's manipulating Noel just like he's manipulating everyone else around here—you especially. He's now told Noel that he is only allowed to speak to the boys—that he doesn't have to 'dance to our tune.' Well, whose tune is he dancing to, then? And Helen, I can't believe you are taking Hamish's demand for the boys to be taught classical studies seriously. Most of these boys can barely read and write, but Hamish clicks his fingers and we run off to provide them with classical studies textbooks, for God's sake!"

Once again Helen found herself trying to forge a middle ground between the warring parties.

"They aren't textbooks as such. They're a set of illustrated mythologies and the boys seem to really like them, especially the Maori boys. Maybe they see similarities with their own mythologies."

"Their mythologies? Give me a break! Most of the Maori boys here haven't a clue who the hell they themselves are, let alone know anything of their own mythologies. Their mythologies are about Snoop Dogg and Tupac. They would love nothing more than to be living in the Bronx."

"What a load of old bollocks!" snapped Helen. "I have verified all that Hamish told us about Victor. Every word is true. It's criminal that we didn't know his academic potential, and as for the others, they know a damn sight more than you think. And even if they don't, they enjoy copying the drawings in those textbooks, and if it keeps them happy, then what's the crime?"

"Look, obviously I support the boys having an interest in the books, but the point is that it's Hamish calling the shots, not us. We're the ones supposed to be in charge, but increasingly it seems to be Hamish," said Simon.

"I'm sorry, I wasn't aware that it was a competition, Simon. What does it matter whose decision it is anyway? The real point is that the boys are showing an interest in books, and I don't know about you, but I think that's bloody amazing!"

"And when Hamish tires of this or decides that the boys are 'too stupid' to do classical studies? What's to say his next educational fancy for the boys won't be something like bomb making for the intellectually challenged or taxidermy for beginners? You've all read the police report on that cheery little incident, I presume? No damn wonder the courts won't let him own pets!"

Terry flashed Simon an angry look. "A low shot!"

"Just telling it how it is, Terry, old chap. And Helen, who gave the go-ahead for him to have his own office?"

"Don't be ridiculous—it's hardly an office. It's little more than a broom cupboard with a desk that was about to be thrown out anyway. It's only a place for him to store

all his books and somewhere quiet to write his journal—
and to cut this gripe session short, I know your next com-
plaint will be about the files. As I said before, we just
have to assume that Hamish can and will gain access to
areas that we have presumed up to now are totally private, and that includes computer files. I suggest we all
change our passwords immediately. It didn't cost much
to change the locks on our private offices and I think it
was a good wake-up call for all of us to be a lot more
vigilant about security."

**Journal Entry 5—July 2**

Now Mrs. Grenville wants me to write about my
childhood. What she really wants is for me to cough up
some interesting insights into how I was beaten up by
my father or felt up by a dirty old man or something. My
first thought was to spin you a load of rubbish about how
a succession of my alcoholic mother's drug-ravaged
boyfriends repeatedly abused me, but no such luck,
Mrs. Grenville!

I had an ordinary family life, living in Whangarei first
and then Wadestown in Wellington. I can't remember
being smacked once by Mum or Dad. Maybe I should
have been, I don't know. For the record: I am an only
child—why have more when you hit the jackpot first

time? (Ha ha!) My father is called Morris (an ordinary name for a very ordinary person!) and he is a business consultant of some sort. I sometimes wind him up by calling him Morris Minor—you know, like the inoffensive little round car. My mother is called Eileen and she's a high school librarian. This can't have paid much, but I reckon it's a much more important job than being a business consultant. Because I was a bit of a disaster at kindergarten, I used to go to the school library with her before I started at my own school. This was great and I would read books all day. I was sort of like a pet for the high school kids and they thought it was funny when I would quiz them on different things I had read and they knew nothing about. I was laughing at them—they were the stupid ones, not me. I can recall being amazed that these kids could get to fourteen or fifteen years of age and not know the difference between, say, a stegosaurus and a triceratops. Some of them had never even heard of Alexander the Great! I am one of those people who reads something once and it sticks in my mind. The older kids would get a real kick out of quizzing me about what I had read and sometimes I would bring the house down by reciting whole pages of stuff. Yeah, little freaky Hamish, off to a good start. How to be a normal kid: Lesson one—don't recite large chunks of teen-targeted books to kids ten years older than you when you are only supposed to be up to *Run, Spot, Run.*

Mum tried numerous times to put me in various types of preschool situations, but after a week or two she would be told not to bring me back. I don't know why, but I suppose I was probably acting too aggressively. I was a climber as well, which used to really freak them out. I can recall climbing to the highest point on the roof in a kindergarten I went to for a week and pissing on top of the kids playing in the sandpit below. (Great! I can almost hear you salivating. "Why does Hamish have this compulsion to urinate on things? Let's analyze this to death!") Anyway, the kids didn't seem to care too much, but the stupid staff went ballistic. I pretended to be too scared to come down, and because the women running the place were too fat and useless to climb up and get me, they had to ring the fire brigade, like I was a dumb cat stuck in a tree. I waited until two firemen had climbed up and were just about to reach for me and then simply jumped down into the sandpit. Some of the kids thought it was pretty cool, but I don't recall any of the adults getting the joke. So, as you can see, nothing unusual anywhere so far.

As I said, I have very ordinary parents who lead very ordinary lives, apart from having me to cope with—I suppose I can be a bit difficult at times. I knew that I was not like other kids from a very young age. Many of the games little kids played seemed pointless to me and I would usually end up by breaking the toys or fighting with the other kids. I can recall getting angry when the other little kids cried so much because it always seemed to me such a pointless and weak thing to do. Lots of little kids cry like stuck pigs—it would really hurt my ears and make me mad. I never cried, of course. I would yell and shout, but never cry.

Sometimes I feel bad about what my parents have had to put up with from me, but then again, they should be proud of some of what I've done because I am much smarter than most of the kids I have ever known. It's probably true to say that most kids are actually pretty stupid. It used to stun me that some kids could sit for hours doing really boring things like dressing up dolls or playing with cars, when I was more interested in smashing the cars up with hammers or pulling the dolls apart to see what was inside them.

I spent most of the time I attended school bored out of my mind. The teachers hated me criticizing them all the time and demanding to be taught interesting stuff. Don't get me wrong, I don't dislike teachers; in fact, teaching is the most important job in the country, but whereas Alexander the Great had Aristotle for a teacher, I was always stuck with Mr. or Mrs. Average. Writing about my childhood is a really big topic and I suppose I'll have to pick out some highlights for you.

## The Kaka Camp

When I was six, we lived in Whangarei, where Dad was doing some work for the oil refinery at Marsden Point. Mum was worried that I had no friends and joined me up to a group called the Kakas, which was sort of like a junior scout group with some seacraft activities thrown in. I actually enjoyed it most of the time and we did some pretty cool stuff, like making little lanterns out of tins and making our own miniature rock pools. I especially liked it when we made these really big fires out of driftwood.

Once we went on an overnight camp to Limestone Island, a small island in Whangarei Harbour. In the afternoon we helped Department of Conservation workers plant native trees (and I won the prize for the fastest and best planter, of course) and in the evening after tea we had a singalong around the campfire. The trouble started when one of the leaders brought out his special blanket to put around his shoulders. He was a sad, fat little man of about forty and he had spent about a hundred years sewing lots of these little badges onto his gray blanket. He was very proud of them, and to be honest, all of us young kids thought they were pretty special too. He said each badge had a story to tell because each one was earned by going to various scouting conventions in New Zealand and even overseas. He proceeded to tell us some incredibly long and tedious stories about some of the badges and then said each of us kids could have a go at wearing his blanket on our shoulders. He put it on each kid's shoulders for about a minute, but when it was getting to where I was sitting, he said that us last boys would have to wait for another day because it was getting really late and we all had to get into the tents and go to sleep. Well, stuff that! I said I wanted my go now and began to get upset, but he just laughed and said that in the morning I could wear it for five minutes.

In the night I crept out of my tent and crawled into his tent. I took ages getting the blanket off him because he kept starting to wake up. Eventually I got it off him and took it out to the fire. I put it around my shoulders and just sat there for a while. I got bored eventually, and for some reason threw it on the embers of the fire. The smoldering blanket made heaps of smoke and the wind blew it into the tents and woke everyone up. The little fat man cried when he saw his burning blanket and called me a crazy little arsehole. Another man had to hold him back to stop him from attacking me. Overreaction or what?! They called my father and said they were bringing me back to the base and he was to collect me immediately. So that was the end of Kakas for me.

## Judo Lessons

My parents decided that I needed an outlet for my anger and enrolled me in judo lessons. Judo is actually very cool, and as you get better at it, you have different-colored belts. The logic and symbolism of this really seemed to appeal to me, as did the tough discipline. The man who took us kids was great and I liked him straightaway because he made us line up very straight and didn't tell us any stupid jokes. He said if we didn't like the first lesson, that was fine by him and we could bugger off. Then he just got on with it and put us in two lines facing each other. Our first test was to simply stand dead still for five minutes. It was disgraceful how few of the stupid kids could do this. He then showed us how to do a basic hip throw and we had turns throwing our opponents. My opponent was a girl who was older, taller and a lot heavier than me. She threw me easily, and then when it was my turn, she used her weight and wouldn't

let me throw her. The instructor told her to ease off
and let me do it, but she said loudly that I was too little
and weak to throw her and she wanted a bigger partner.
I can't recall doing it, but apparently I punched her in
her big mouth and made her lip bleed. As she fell to the
ground, I grabbed a fistful of her hair and pulled it so
hard that a huge chunk came out in my hand. I wasn't
allowed back again.

## Calf Club

At one stage up north I went to a very small country
school for a while. The biggest thing in the school year
was Calf Club Day, where on a set Saturday, kids would
bring their farm pets to school for this intense
competition and all the parents would come to watch.
We also had to spend hours making these country craft
things, like miniature farms—very boring. Mum thought
I might fit into the school better if I had a pet to enter
into these competitions, so she arranged for us to have a
lamb for a fortnight prior to the competition day to allow
me to get used to leading it and calling it. It was a very
cool lamb so I named it Alexander (of course) and it
learned to walk around on a leash and would come
when called and everything. It's kind of sad that
reasonably smart lambs end up as incredibly stupid

sheep. In the actual competition we had to walk our animals around a sort of obstacle course and then we had to take it off the leash and walk away for a bit and call it. Alexander was good on the first bit but pretty crap on the calling part. He got kind of put off by all the other people and the noise. I could handle that, but what I couldn't handle was the judges giving the best junior lamb award to this kid who cheated. The boy had obviously not fed his scrawny lamb for ages and I saw him give it little bits of bread just before the calling part, so of course the lamb ran straight up to him. The dumb judges wouldn't listen to me when I told them that the kid must be disqualified for cheating. He got a big cup for a prize. What happened next is a bit of a blur, but apparently I kicked the lamb, punched the kid and ran away with the cup. When the teachers found me, I had smashed the cheat's cup to bits. I didn't fit into the school very well after that so I changed to a city school.

## Cross-country

I'm good at most sports but never seem to last long in team sport situations. I usually end up being dropped because I get too angry with my teammates or the coaches for being useless. The best sport for me was long-distance running, and one year I decided to win the Wellington primary schools cross-country title. I trained seriously for six weeks and became super-fit. The problem was, I had just finished reading up about the first-ever marathon back in ancient Greece. A Greek soldier ran hardout from Marathon to Athens, a distance of twenty-six miles, to tell the news of victory over the Persians, and then he collapsed and died. I loved the selfless heroism of this gesture and was determined to do something similar. I think I was intrigued by the idea of pushing your body to the stage of collapse and wondered what it would feel like.

Of course I won the race, but it was only a measly five kilometers long, on a trail around the Mount Victoria town belt. When I crossed the finish line first, I still felt strong so I decided to just keep on running. It was quite funny seeing the looks on the officials' faces when I didn't stop. I ran all the way through town to the Ngauranga Gorge, about fifteen kilometers away, and decided to keep running until I collapsed with exhaustion or died, like the first man to run the marathon.

Trouble was, I was too fit, and my body just refused to collapse. By the time I got to the top of the gorge, I was getting pretty stuffed, but my legs were still working so I kept going. I was getting really slow by the time I got near Porirua, but I was determined to go until I actually collapsed or died. The police eventually stopped me not far from the Paremata roundabout and unfortunately I was too knackered to run away from them. I did sort of collapse as I was forcibly put into their car and driven back to my parents' place in Wadestown. I was partially successful. The cops were pretty good about it and thought I was "a bit of a hero." They even stopped at a dairy and bought me a big drink and a Memphis Meltdown ice cream. Most other people thought I was totally crazy and it even made the newspaper the next day. If there is a kid who has been in the papers more than me, I'm yet to meet him! The story made out that I was some kind of fruitcake, whereas I thought I was bravely pushing the boundaries of twelve-year-old endurance.

There are lots more things like this I could say, but I get kind of sad writing about them. I think I am the only child in New Zealand, or maybe the world, that is not allowed by the courts to own any sort of pets. I am not going to tell you why (it's not because of the rat experiments) because it is quite embarrassing to write about, partly because I can now see that it was a dumb thing to do and partly because it didn't happen when I was a child—I was actually thirteen. Okay, I will just tell you a little bit because I can almost hear your sick groans of disappointment, and I bet you have read distorted versions of what happened in the papers. Before I continue, I want to say that I really like animals. Mind you, if I was a judge, I think I would probably ban me from owning pets too.

## Animal Experiments

I have only attended regular schools for a combined total of five years. This is because I keep getting thrown out of them and end up having to do correspondence lessons from home or in wonderfully enlightened institutions of higher learning like this place. Mind you, it does mean that I can work at my own pace, which is a lot faster than the schools I went to. One hassle I do have, however, is with science subjects like biology that require a certain amount of practical work. There was no way I was going to miss out on this, so I pestered Morris Minor to set up a science laboratory in the garage. To be fair to him, he did a great job. I had a large workbench, sinks and a decent range of chemicals and equipment. He even installed a Bunsen burner fed by an LPG cylinder. The part of biology I was most interested in was dissecting animals, but after the rat experiment episode my parents refused to buy me any more rats, so

I had to improvise. I began by scouring the streets for recent roadkill, but after a week all I found was one very dead cat, which smelled so bad when I cut it up that I vomited, and a couple of semi-dry and rather flat possums. I discovered that if you put Vicks VapoRub under your nose, smells aren't so bad. Eventually I decided that if I was to really understand anatomy, I needed to be dissecting freshly dead animals.

This next stuff is going to sound really bad, but you have to understand that I did try my best to find suitable specimens. My education was at stake here, so I had to be inventive. No one makes a big fuss when high school biology students all over the country cut up animals by the thousands. Anyway, one of our neighbors was like a major breeder of miniature poodles, and these dogs, like their owners for some reason, seemed to hate me with a passion. I guess the owners had a bit of a reason to hate me because of the burned-down garage (talk about holding a grudge!), but I can't recall giving their stupid dogs a reason to bark like demented demons every time they saw me. I decided that one less yapping poodle would be no great loss to the world, and one day when the neighbors had gone out, I lured the boldest one, with the unlikely name of Caesar, to the fence with a bit of meat. I grabbed it, and holding its mouth shut so it couldn't yap, I took it to my laboratory, where I had set up a humane animal disposal unit. Actually it was an old fish tank that I had converted to a gas chamber. The dog had an incredibly strong grip on life and took almost five minutes to die—quite surprising, really. This set me off on a long and interesting series of thoughts about how strong the survival instinct is and what is the exact moment that life ceases—is life over when the heart stops or when the brain dies? Neither, really, because people have been resuscitated well after the heart has stopped pumping, and with modern technology, brain-dead people can be kept alive for ages. Maybe religious people are on to something when they go on about us having a soul and we only die when the soul leaves the body. Unfortunately I couldn't spend more time on these engrossing issues because I had work to do. I was just about to start cutting the dog up and examining its heart and lungs, which was what I was interested in, when I had an idea. I'm not sure why I thought of this, but I decided on a great practical joke. How cool would it be if I stuffed the dead dog, I mean properly, like a taxidermist, and then put it back in their yard in a natural sort of pose?

I Googled *taxidermy* and was surprised at how many books and videos you can buy on stuffing and preserving animals—very weird. There sure are some crazy people out there. There was this joke site called Taxidermy for Beginners, where two American idiots give the basics of how to stuff a mouse. I kind of adapted their procedures for a larger animal. Using a very sharp scalpel, you have to kind of ease the whole skin off the animal, being ultra-careful not to cut or rip through the pelt. I followed their advice and made the first incision in the back between the shoulder blades, not along the stomach, where it is much easier to make mistakes, and then carefully cut right along the back to the start of the tail. The legs were tricky and I decided to leave the bones in, although breaking them at the top joint was more difficult than I anticipated. The eyes were the hardest because I had to carefully cut away the tissue and the masses of little veins that attach the eye to the skull. I got quite sad doing this because it sort of hit me how incredibly complicated a life-form is. I mean, here was this dog that I had thought was just an annoying nuisance, yet every part of it was stunningly constructed. The eyes were so complex and each little blood vessel and each piece of nerve tissue was so beautiful and perfect. It was quite a spiritual feeling in a way and I felt grateful to the dog for giving me this new perspective on life (the judge didn't share my feelings, unfortunately). To cut a long story short, I ended up with an empty dog skin that I had to fill and shape. The first filling I tried was cotton wool wrapped around a wire frame, but it went soggy and looked very unrealistic. I was glad I hadn't sewn it up like that because it looked ridiculous.

I ended up using some roofing insulation that Dad had stored in the garage because it retains its springiness so well. I decided to go for an alert pose, head up and one foot raised like a pointer spaniel, and before inserting the shaped frame into the dog skin, I worked for hours to get it just right. The final step was to sew the pelt together and I used thin fishing nylon for this. I don't like to boast, but I think it ended up looking very realistic and I thought that although the owners would be upset when they found their missing dog, they would be pleased at the trouble someone had gone to. All this took much longer than I thought it would and by the late afternoon the stuffed dog was giving off a distinctly unpleasant smell, as were the leftover body parts, which I stuffed into a plastic trash bag. A real taxidermist would have cured the skin with some sort of chemical to stop rot setting in. Two noises alerted me to the time—Mum calling me in for tea and the neighbors calling loudly for their little Caesar. Of course, they made a huge fuss over the missing dog and spent all that night scouring the area for it—a bit excessive considering they had four more at home. It was a bit more understandable when Mum said the missing dog was a national champion for its breed. Well, how was I to know that?

Early the next morning I brushed up Caesar's coat, which had gone kind of limp (and stinky!) overnight, crept into their yard and placed him on the lawn, looking up toward the house. To make the discovery better, I hid in our garage and made some loud yapping noises. The woman opened the door and screamed with joy when she saw the dog looking up at her from the bottom of the yard. She ran down the steps so fast she stumbled and her husband had to help her up. I kind of got into the feeling too and felt really happy for her as she ran toward Caesar, forgetting for a moment that she was soon going to get the shock of her life—which she did.

I owned up the same morning because I was mature enough to realize that I was responsible for her collapse and subsequent stroke, and I could see that my joke wasn't really all that funny. The annoying thing was that no matter how much I apologized, people were just not going to let this one go and I ended up in the Youth Court again charged with about a million offenses. Of course, the news-starved media got on the game as well and there was a story about me being the same boy that killed the Iraqi man and about how mentally deranged and dangerous I was and why wasn't there a specialist place for young loonies like me, etc., etc. So I hope you are all satisfied now—and yes, Mrs. Grenville, every word here is true.

The big question everyone wants the answer to is why I do so many strange, violent things. All I can say is that I get pushed into doing violent things by stuff that happens around me. People treat me like some sort of freak, probably because I'm much smarter than them and bum them out so much. I don't know. I used to think that I only did these things when people didn't treat me fairly, but sometimes I do them just because it feels right. I am old enough now to know that lots of the things I do are not acceptable, like the taxidermy experiment. And despite what all of you think, I do have an understanding of how my actions impact on others. Whether I care about what other people think is another matter. I actually get quite depressed about all this at times because I also know that I will probably keep doing these things. All I know is that they feel exactly right at the time.

It seems to me that I was born in the wrong time period and in the wrong setting. I'm quite jealous of people born into warrior societies or in times of lengthy warfare. My ultimate dream is to be able to spend several years on some sort of glorious military campaign, fighting against tough, devious opponents and suffering unimaginable hardships—all for glory and valour, like the early Crusaders, for example. Man, I would like to see someone like the Gestapo try to get military secrets out of me! They could perform as many horrible tortures as they could think of and I would laugh and spit in their faces! I guess this is why I love Alexander the Great so much. He is the ultimate hero, combining huge intelligence and vision on the one hand with unusual guts and raw courage on the other. He was the ultimate military leader and conquered most of the known world, leading from the front and suffering alongside his men. He was probably responsible for hundreds of thousands of deaths, some historians say 750,000. And how is he remembered today? Alexander the Brutal? Alexander the Freak? Alexander the Sadistic Psycho? No way—he is simply referred to as Alexander the Great. How do you think he would get on today?

I think he'd get a hard time like me and be regarded as
a dangerous lunatic.

I also regret not being born in the 1920s so that I
could go and fight in World War Two alongside my
second main man, Charles Upham. Here is a little bit
about his background—if I write too much, a certain
person with limited appreciation of historically
important people will have a big freak out!

### A Little Bit About Charles Upham

Charles Upham was born in Christchurch in 1921 to
a middle-class family, but he did not want to be a
professional man like his father; he wanted to be a
farmer. When he left school, he became a shepherd,
but as soon as New Zealand found itself at war with
Germany, he was one of the first to enlist. Although he
was no good at parade ground drills and usually looked
scruffy, he became expert with various weapons,
especially hand grenades. For the intelligent people
reading this journal, I will include a bit more about him
later, especially about how he came to be awarded not
one but two Victoria Crosses.

I think I have been tested for just about every
disorder known to man, and the experts say they can't
tell exactly what my problem is. For ages they thought I

was autistic, like that idiot kid in a book I was made to read at the last boys' home. He finds a dead dog on the lawn with a garden fork stuck through it and decides to find out who was responsible. I'm definitely not like him. What a loser! Actually, I quite like autistic people. They have this great ability to focus on things. Only problem is, they don't know when to stop focusing on things. That's not like me because I can stop whenever I like. I can sense certain people smirking at that comment, thinking that I am a classic case of an obsessive person, but I know I'm not. Other genius child psychologists have concluded I'm some sort of sociopath with a hatred of people in general. Wrong—I only hate stupid people, and they don't seem to have a smart medical term for this "disorder."

There was one almost interesting therapist at Warburton Boys' Home who said I had definite misogynist tendencies, claiming that I resorted to violence more quickly when being challenged by women than by men. She also questioned why none of my heroes were women. When I said this is because women lack the ruthless courage of men, she disagreed and suggested I do some research on Joan of Arc, and I have to admit she had a good point. Joan certainly meets my three main heroic criteria. She was a good military strategist, she was physically tough and she was certainly over-the-top brave, especially when she was being burned at the stake. I still have one big stumbling block with her, though, and that is to do with the "voices and visions" she had from Saint Catherine and Saint Michael, telling her, a little peasant girl, to lead the French armies against the English and throw them back over the English Channel. What is it about little French peasant girls and these heavenly visitations? First Joan in 1425, and then in 1858 in the town of Lourdes in the south of France, little Bernadette Soubirous is minding her own business, looking after the goats and doing other regular peasant girl stuff, when along comes the Virgin Mary and stuffs up her life good and proper. You never hear of little peasant boys being accosted by pushy saints while out in the fields. I think I might have admitted Joan into my team if it hadn't been for the stuff about the visitations. She could have just said, "Listen up, people. The English are a bunch of bastards and we need to get our shit together to force them out of the country. If none of you pussies are willing to get this under way, then I, Joan the maid, will lead the way!" Mind you, who would have listened to a little peasant girl back then anyway? She probably had to invent the religious angle so they would take her seriously—who knows?

The last child psychologist I endured came up with the startling conclusion that I was a lot smarter than average and this was causing me social adjustment problems. No shit, Sherlock!!

# 101
# CHAPTER
# SIX

Seven thirty in the morning. Toko Wihongi looked hard at the sixteen boys lined up in front of him on the back rugby paddock: eight Maori, three Pacific Island and five Pakeha boys, one of whom was Hamish. Toko had been planning to run this course for some time and now felt that the mix of boys was right. He persuaded the other staff that learning how to use a *taiaha* was not just useful for Maori boys. It could teach all the boys a lot about themselves, as well as encouraging self-discipline. Every boy on the course had a long history of violence. Like the other boys, Hamish was stripped down to a pair of black rugby shorts, and he shivered in the weak winter sun.

"I have selected you boys for taiaha training, firstly

because you all need to learn discipline and respect, and secondly because I can see something in each of you. In some of you it's not much, but each of you has something I can work with. You boys all think you're tough, eh? But all you know is one kind of toughness and it's not enough. When I look at you, I can see that most of you are marshmallow inside. You need inner toughness. Some of you are even having real trouble right now just standing still listening to me. I know it's cold, but so what? You Maori boys—you think our ancestors ran around in winter wearing wool jerseys and hoodies? You beat the cold by not giving in to it, so just stand still and look straight at me. Over the next two weeks we'll see how tough you really are. We're going to practice for two hours every day. You are going to be stiff and bloody sore tomorrow, but you are going to line up just like this and not moan about it. I know that you're all dying to get stuck into learning the moves, but the first thing we have to learn is what the parts of the taiaha are called."

Several of the boys moaned. Toko glared at them and said, "The next weakling who complains is off the course!" He held the taiaha over his head before continuing. "This isn't a bloody stick, you know. The taiaha is sacred. You are privileged to have this opportunity and you will learn to name the parts correctly and treat the taiaha with respect. If you are too gutless to handle that, you can bugger off right now!" The moaners shuffled and looked embarrassed.

"Okay, then, no more moaning. When I point to each part, I will say the name and you will all say it after me. No one leaves this spot until every one of you can name all seven parts. Is that clear? I said, is that clear?"

"Yes, Mr. Wihongi!" shouted sixteen boys.

"I will say them all together first, starting at the top, then we'll work on each one. *Te arero* . . ."

"*Te arero!*" shouted Leu, a heavyset Samoan boy.

"Hey, boy!" said Toko angrily. "Open your ears up. I said that I would say them all first, and then you all say them, one by one, after me. Those flaps on your head aren't just to make you pretty, they're called ears. Okay, I'll start again. *Te arero, nga whatu, te upoko, te awe, te tinana, te ate, te rau.*"

Twenty minutes later, the boys had amazed themselves. Each boy could now clearly name each part and pronounce them almost as well as Toko.

Toko smiled. "*Tino pai, tino pai.* Now we can get down to learning how to use the taiaha. I have sixteen taiaha here. You will come forward one at a time and select yours. But don't just take any old one. Look carefully before you choose. They look the same, but each one is different. Each has a spirit—a *wairua*. The taiaha will choose you as well. You will know when you have the one for you, because it will feel right in your hands. And taiaha don't like being grabbed at. They like you to approach quietly and respectfully. When you have the one for you, it will sit just right in your hands and you will feel its wairua flow into your arms. Hey, Raymond, don't smirk. I'm telling you the truth. Go and see for yourself. You can be the first one to choose."

Toko's talk had the desired effect. Raymond made quite a procedure of holding various taiaha until he found one he liked.

"This is the one for me, Mr. Wihongi. It feels just right, eh."

Soon each boy was proudly holding his own carefully chosen taiaha and was more than ready to begin work.

For two hours the boys worked hard at the moves, stopping only twice for drink breaks. Each dropped taiaha resulted in twenty push-ups and lots of ribbing from the others, which Toko tolerated and at points even encouraged. They learned fast and Toko had to admit to a sense of pride in his charges. For several of them this represented the longest time they had ever spent on a physical task.

"*Werohia!*" he shouted, and all fourteen boys lunged

forward, shouting back in unison. At the command *"Poua upoko!"* they swung their taiaha at the air. When Toko called *"Mangopare!"* the boys blocked imaginary attacks, and when he shouted *"Karo waewae pourua!"* they leapt forward as if to strike their foe.

"We are going to finish off by sparring in pairs. I will call the moves and you are to attack or block accordingly, but it will be in slow motion and there will be no contact at all. Is that clear?"

"Yes, Mr. Wihongi!" the boys shouted, now used to replying in unison.

"You are to stop all blows well before any contact point. Okay, then. First I will demonstrate the speed I mean, and then I will pair you off and tell you whether you are attacking or defending. Victor, I think you must have done a little of this before, eh? You come and be my opponent."

Everyone watched carefully as Toko and Victor went through all the moves they had covered, taking turns to be attacker and defender. With one more warning from Toko about non-contact they began.

Hamish, in the defense role, found himself paired with Raymond Maihi, the large and usually amiable court-jester of the group. On Toko's command, the attacking line moved forward and slowly swung at their foes, all of whom slowly parried the blows and moved back. For about ten minutes all went well, but an angry shout from Raymond broke the group's concentration.

"Ah, shit, you've cut my hand, you dick!" Raymond snapped. He rushed forward, forgetting Toko's warnings about contact.

Hamish stood his ground, then deftly sidestepped Raymond, cracking him on the jaw with the taiaha as he thundered past. Instantly the other boys rushed over and formed a circle to watch, but Toko was in the center before it closed and he held the two boys apart.

"Did either of you two idiots listen to a word I said?" he shouted, his face red with anger.

"He's a defender, but he stabbed my hand!" Raymond snarled, straining against Toko's hold.

"Only because you were so crap at the moves. You're lucky I didn't stab you in your fat *puku*!"

Somehow this broke the tension and the other boys laughed. "Jeez, that Hamish fulla's a hard case, eh?" Leu commented.

Toko was still fuming, though.

"You're both off the course until further notice. Give me your taiaha and stand on opposite sides of the field until we finish. Go on—move!"

The fight had drained from Raymond by this time and

he sullenly surrendered his taiaha and walked off. However, Hamish had other ideas.

"No, I want to keep going with another partner."

"Like bloody hell you will! This isn't a counseling session, boy. You'll do exactly as I say!" Toko moved forward to grasp the taiaha, but Hamish leapt back out of range and adopted an aggressive stance. Toko was stunned at his cheek.

"So, after a couple of hours you think you have the mana to attack me with your taiaha. Give it to me now, or I'll kick your backside so hard, you won't sit down for a week!"

Hamish moved back several more paces and maintained his stance.

Several of the boys began to murmur angrily. They respected Toko, and this *porangi* Pakeha kid was shaming him out.

"Give it to him, Hamish. Stop being a dick, just give it to him!" Victor commanded.

But Hamish was having none of it and held his ground. Victor had suddenly had enough and rushed forward to grab Hamish's taiaha. At the same time Hamish swung the weapon in a tight, vicious arc directly at Victor's head. The move was lightning fast. Toko instinctively lunged forward. His raised left arm blocked the blow, stopping it from smashing into Victor's head, but his elbow took the full force of Hamish's taiaha. He fell to one knee and clutched his shattered arm while the boys stared, all openmouthed. No one moved. Toko slowly got to his feet and turned to Hamish. Color had drained from his face and his breath was short and ragged, but he spoke deliberately and clearly.

"Victor, go to the shed and bring me two lengths of baling twine. Go on! Hurry up, boy! The rest of you step back ten paces and do not move."

The boys moved back in one body, as if this were part of their training. They were very quiet. Toko and Hamish stared at each other in silence. Victor returned shortly with the twine and held it toward Toko.

"Right, tie the two pieces together and then tie my broken arm tightly to my body so it can't move."

"Yeah? But you've got some bone coming through." Victor looked over to his mates. "Hey, look, youse fullas, Mr. Wihongi's got some bits of broken bone sticking through his skin!"

"Just tie it and hurry up!" Toko gasped. He shuddered with pain as Victor did his best to immobilize his badly fractured elbow. When it was done, Toko marched up to Hamish and said, "Your blow was powerful enough to have killed Victor. You have broken my arm. Now it will be my turn. My *utu*. You can make one move only and that is to raise your left arm, as I did, to stop the taiaha from caving in your skull. If you are too slow, or if your arm is too weak to stop me, then the top of your skull will lift off like an eggshell. Do you understand what I am saying to you?"

Hamish held Toko's gaze. "I understand," he replied.

Hamish then stood to attention and stared directly ahead. The other boys looked at each other uneasily. Mr. Wihongi was tough and a bit crazy, but he wouldn't kill the kid, surely? Nah, he's just having him on, eh?

Toko walked to within three meters of Hamish and began to slowly swing his taiaha, trying to establish some sort of one-armed rhythm and working out his aim and distance.

"Hey, Mr. Wihongi," Raymond blurted, "it was all my fault really—you don't have to kill him. Just rough him up a bit, just . . . just give him a hiding! We can help you if you like."

"Yeah," added another, "he's just an out-of-it Pakeha kid and if you kill him, you'll have to go to jail for ages and ages."

"All of you shut up and stand still. This is between me and Hamish!"

Toko shifted rapidly from foot to foot and moved closer,

flicking his heels backward and breathing in short, explosive bursts. When he was within striking distance, he reached the taiaha slowly forward and touched the blade lightly against Hamish's head, just above his left ear. Toko drew the weapon back and with a loud shout of pain swung it forward as powerfully as he could. The blade passed so close to Hamish's forehead that it actually collected a tuft of hair on the way past. The strength of the blow carried Toko forward so that he ended up almost nose to nose with Hamish, as if they were about to *hongi*. Toko stared fiercely at the boy, and then his eyes softened.

"You haven't moved a muscle! Why didn't you move back or try to block me?" Toko asked.

"I didn't want to."

"You are either very brave or very stupid, Hamish Graham. How did you know that I would miss?"

"I didn't. I thought I was going to die. I was ready for it, but I think you missed on purpose. Why didn't you kill me? You had the right to kill me."

"Because this isn't your time to die." Toko looked calmly at Hamish, then moved back a pace and looked at the other boys.

"No one is to speak of what happened here. What you will say is that it was my fault. Say I lost my concentration and walked into Victor's taiaha during training. It was an accident. Okay with that, Victor? You're the biggest, so they'll believe that. I'll make sure you're not in any trouble. There will be a two-day break from taiaha training until my arm is set and then we continue. Is that clear?"

"Yes, Mr. Wihongi!" they all shouted.

Toko swayed and would have fallen if Hamish had not leapt forward to hold him up.

"I'm sorry that I mucked up your training session and I'm sorry I broke your arm."

"I know you are, boy. Here, you and Victor can help me back to the changing shed. Leu, run back and tell them I'll need a lift to the hospital."

It was a strangely subdued group of boys who gathered for tea that night.

## Journal Entry 6—July 20

I think I will be moving again soon. Terry and Mrs. Grenville deny anything's up, but I can tell by the way the others are looking at me that I'm not wanted. Mr. Whittle is up front about it at least. He told me that he doesn't believe for one second that Mr. Wihongi broke his arm accidentally and that the sooner I'm gone, the better. He reckoned I will have to go to some sort of secure psychiatric hospital because I am a danger to myself and others. Yeah, whatever.

Well, since you all seem to know anyway, then yes, it was me that broke Mr. Wihongi's arm. Yep, crazy old Hamish. I was trying to take Victor's head off, but Mr. Wihongi stuck his arm out. He's the man. I reckon he's wasted working with broken kids. I think something must have gone wrong for him in the army. I mean, why would a guy like that want to come here? I bet he was an awesome soldier, like I know I would be. If there was a real war on, people wouldn't call me crazy; they'd call me a hero.

It was a weird feeling, standing waiting for Mr. Wihongi to kill me with the taiaha. He had the right to kill me, of course, and it felt kind of peaceful waiting for him to do it. Waiting for death can be peaceful if your killer has the right to kill you. Part of me would go into him. That's a bit like cannibalism.

I have a lot of time for the old Maori warriors. Many of them were awesome military strategists and some were incredibly brutal. I think that the best of them all was Te Rauparaha. One time, Te Rauparaha and about twenty family members were invited to a feast by a Manawatu *iwi,* but it was a trap. Late at night they were attacked and although Te Rauparaha escaped, several of his children were killed. He came back shortly after with a larger force and destroyed the village. He is supposed to have personally killed 200 prisoners by smashing their skulls with his *mere*. Don't know if this is true or not. Lots of things I have read about him sound pretty far-fetched. Apparently they were all just lined up in a long row and stood there waiting their turn. I reckon they would have felt a bit like I felt waiting for Mr. Wihongi to kill me. Being killed by a man like Te Rauparaha, for a good reason, is a noble way to go. Awesome.

I reckon that Te Rauparaha is one of the most important figures in New Zealand history and everyone should know a lot more about him. So, Mrs. Grenville and you others, like it or not, here is some stuff you should know about him.

### Things You Should Know About Te Rauparaha

Te Rauparaha was born in 1768 at Kawhia, into a *rangatira* class of the Ngati Toa tribe, which meant he was special from birth, but like Alexander, he had to compete with his siblings to make a mark. There are other similarities with Alexander as well. He was a little below average height but way above average intelligence and was fiercely ambitious. His mother,

Parekohatu, and his father, Werawera, nicknamed their mischievous youngest son Maui Potiki, because like his namesake he was always getting into trouble. He was such an ultra-smart boy that in about 1780 he was sent away to Maketu for five years' study at a school for leaders called Whare Wananga. At this school he would have been taught a wide variety of subjects and skills—not by writing things down like in our system, but by listening and discussion. He would have studied genealogy, legends and mythology, the gods, philosophy, military tactics, history, botany, astronomy, and martial arts—particularly with taiaha, mere and *patu*. Although the setting and context are totally different, it is clear to me that he and Alexander the Great had very similar educations as well.

Many early Pakeha who came across Te Rauparaha were astonished at the extent of his knowledge and the ease with which he adopted new knowledge. Mind you, they probably had him labeled as the noble-savage type. Even today he tends to be remembered mostly as a brutal warrior, but he was also a thinker and was quite intellectual. That's why I rank him up there with Alexander.

When he was seventeen, he married a beautiful fifteen-year-old girl called Marore and the tribe held a special feast in his honor. At these feasts the guests of honor were given special small food treats, or *kinaki,* along with the main part of their meals. These might take the form of a choice cut of meat from a pig or a very tender baby fern root—or even sometimes a piece of flesh from a fallen enemy. At the feast there was an accidental oversight and his young wife did not get any sort of kinaki. Te Rauparaha saw an opportunity in this and decided to be hugely offended. He knew that they had no high-ranking prisoners at this time, but he demanded that his young wife be given the freshly cooked flesh of an enemy chief to eat. He said that his mana had been trampled, and he made such a fuss that the tribal leaders allowed him to take a *taua,* or raiding party, and attack one of their Waikato enemies. He made a bold but very carefully planned attack on the enemy tribe's *pa,* and in the ensuing battle Te Rauparaha personally killed four men. He returned victorious with many prisoners, the foremost of whom was a chief called Te Haunga. Unfortunately for Te Haunga, he was killed and eaten the next day, proving to be a very fitting kinaki for Te Rauparaha's young wife.

Maybe what separates great leaders from good leaders is the ability to identify opportunities and to act on them without hesitation. Te Rauparaha could easily have overlooked the missing kinaki—it wasn't really such a big deal—but he instantly saw an opportunity to stamp his mark on his people. Alexander saw a similar opportunity when he broke the wild stallion. Like Te Rauparaha, he could easily have been killed acting on the opportunity, but the rewards were immense and both men knew they had to act fast and with complete confidence.

People often say how hard it must have been for the Maori living in those times. I don't believe it. I would give my eyeteeth to have been one of Te Rauparaha's warriors in that raiding party. I made Morris Minor take me to Kawhia one holiday when I was eleven, just to see where Te Rauparaha came from, and it's a choice place with great beaches and forests. In Te Rauparaha's time the ocean and the forest provided all the food they needed, and whenever they wanted to, they could get together a raiding party and go to war. Awesome!

Things ended up getting pretty hot for Te Rauparaha, and pressure from Te Wherowhero, the first Maori king, forced him to make a strategic withdrawal from the area. He had lots of close calls during this period, including the time in 1821 when Ngati Te Aho warriors were close on his tail and cornered him in a village near Te Rapa. He only escaped by hiding in a food pit while

Te Wharerangi's wife sat over the entrance doing some domestic chore. This is supposed to be when he composed his famous *haka,* "Ka Mate, Ka Mate." I'm not really sure why the All Blacks used this haka for so long. Sure, it's a great haka, but it was composed for a specific occasion by a warrior who was actually despised by a lot of Maori of the time and still is by their descendants in some of the areas he terrorized. The new All Black haka, "Kapa o Pango," is much better. I love the throat-slashing bit and I get annoyed when it is sometimes watered down to a sort of lame chest scratch. I am thinking of writing to All Black management and suggesting they use a red dye to make it look like the players are actually drawing blood during this part of the haka. They could use skin-colored blood sachets attached to their necks. I reckon that would really rattle the opposition, seeing a team prepared to draw their own blood before the game even started. Bet they won't be allowed to do it, though.

Te Rauparaha ended up taking his combined Ngati Toa and Ngati Raukawa warriors down to the Kapiti coast, where he set up camp on Kapiti Island and held it against all attackers for years, including in 1824, when six tribes from the lower North Island and the upper South Island combined to launch one last attempt to

flush him out. Te Rauparaha lured them into making
their landing at Waiorua Bay, an area he knew he could
defend with his much smaller army. The combined force
suffered a crushing defeat and then Te Rauparaha's
warriors chased the survivors back to the mainland,
killing heaps more in the process. Way to go,
Te Rauparaha!

Te Rauparaha was also an astute businessman, and
many European sailing ships of the time sailed to his
island fortress to trade muskets, rum, tools and other
such things for flax, greenstone and maybe preserved
heads and the services of slave women. It's hard to
verify these sorts of claims because Te Rauparaha got
bad press from European settlers who tended to paint
him as a vicious and cunning savage only interested in
pillage and slaughter. Maybe these stories were spread
by land-grabbing Europeans, especially from the New
Zealand Company, as a way of deflecting attention from
themselves. Who knows?

Somehow he ended up being a widely respected
character and even provided materials and labor for the
building of a church called Rangiatea, which survived
for 146 years until it was destroyed by fire in 1995. So, as
you can see, he was an amazing guy and well deserving
of his place in my very select crew.

I have been to most places where Te Rauparaha hung out and one day I intend going to Greece and seeing every place that Alexander and his army marched to. This might take some time because I suppose I will have to do it on horseback or on foot to make it authentic.

I've been talking to Mr. Wihongi quite a lot lately. I tell him about my main men, and as you know by now they are Alexander the Great, Charles Upham and Te Rauparaha. He tells me stuff about his childhood—he's Ngati Porou, like Victor. This could be part of the odd connection they seem to have I suppose. He had really on-to-it parents who sent him to Te Aute College, where he was a good scholar and captain of the rugby team's First XV in his last year. He also tells me about being in the army. Only thing he won't tell me is why he left it. I'll find out, though, because I am very good at getting information I want. Most of our talks are private, but here is one example I can write about. For an army guy he doesn't know as much as he should about the great World War Two hero, Charles Upham, so I told him about how brave he was and how I reckon Upham must have been a bit crazy like me and really tough like him. A wicked combination. I said earlier I would let you know a bit more about him, so here goes. And I know that you're probably moaning again, Mrs. Grenville, but too bad. You need to know some more about Charles Upham.

## More About Charles Upham

Upham was the only combat soldier to be awarded the Victoria Cross twice—once for bravery in Crete and the other time for bravery in North Africa. The Poms, who awarded these medals, were as stingy as hell with them, especially when it came to New Zealand and Australian soldiers, who I reckon they looked down on, so to get it twice was totally amazing. I have now been to the Waiouru Army Museum four times to see his medals and think that all proud Kiwis should make this pilgrimage before they die. To stand in the Valour Alcove in the museum and to be just a thin plate of glass away from these treasures is a total blast. I just love visiting that place.

There was one time in Crete when Upham returned alone to a fight scene to rescue a wounded soldier, despite being wounded in the shoulder by shrapnel and being shot through the foot. He was only a little guy, but he carried the soldier back over his good shoulder, all the time being clearly visible to enemy snipers. Another time he was on his way to warn other troops that they were about to be overtaken by rapidly advancing

German soldiers when he ended up being cut off himself. He was wounded yet again and collapsed, feigning death. When two soldiers approached, he staggered to his feet, shot them both dead and eventually staggered back to his own platoon. And then there was the time he and his platoon had to recapture this important airfield at a place called Maleme. They met stiff resistance from tough German troops all the way and yet again Upham was wounded. He told one of his men to cut out the shrapnel with a pocketknife. Imagine that, just standing there while bits of metal are being dug out of your flesh with a pocketknife.

But I reckon his bravest moment came in Egypt when the New Zealand Division was receiving a real hammering from General Rommel's tanks. Rommel had cleverly encircled the New Zealand division troops and began to close the net on them. Upham, who was a captain by this time, rallied the troops and to the Germans' surprise led a foot charge on the nearest tanks, destroying one by jumping onto it and shoving a grenade through the hatch. This action was instrumental in allowing the New Zealand division to break through the enemy lines and escape.

Upham's luck eventually ran out, though, and he was captured and sent to Weinsberg prisoner of war camp.

He made four escape attempts from this camp and so he was sent to Colditz prison camp, which was a camp for the toughest prisoners. On the way there he actually leapt out of a speeding train. The dumb guards allowed him to go into the toilet cubicle unattended, and once inside, he smashed the glass in a small window and threw his pack and army greatcoat out into the night. Because he was quite little, he managed to squeeze through himself. He was knocked unconscious by the fall but came around eventually and searched for a couple of hours before finding his pack and coat. He was on the run for forty-eight hours before being recaptured. I used to have this really wicked recurring dream in which Upham and I are on the run from the Germans and we go through all sorts of unimaginable hardships to avoid being recaptured. We travel at night and hide out in the day, sometimes clinging together in the freezing-cold winter conditions to stay alive. I once made the big mistake of telling a boy at school who I thought I could trust about this dream. Next thing I knew, the wanker has gone and told half the school that I have wet dreams about sleeping with some old soldier. He didn't think it was so funny when I smashed his stupid face in. It was one of those occasions when I lost it totally and had to be hauled off him by two big Year 13 boys.

What the fuck would he know about someone like Upham? I am getting that angry noise in my head even thinking about this stuff so I will have to stop typing for a while until I calm down. Okay, I'm feeling better now. It's just that anything bad said about Captain Upham or any sort of desecration of his valor makes me a bit crazy.

Considering all his escape attempts, many people are amazed that Upham wasn't killed by his captors, but I think they must have had a big respect for him. They knew quality when they saw it. Now you can see why he is one of my favorite heroes. What a man! If you ask me, those young men who went off to war were the lucky ones. They got an awesome adventure and the chance to see just what they were capable of. Man, I'm so jealous of those guys. The nearest I can get to them is by attending Anzac Day ceremonies—and yes, I have attended dawn parade every year since I was five. Well, I did miss one, because I was in another boys' home and the cretins who ran it wouldn't let me attend. I made them pay for that, believe me!

Yeah, yeah—I know what you're thinking. Stupid little Hamish—he doesn't understand about the real horrors of war. Well, obviously I haven't been in a real war, but I understand more than you think. There was this one well-meaning English teacher I had who didn't relate at all well to my opinions about war. He made me read several war poems by a World War One poet called Wilfred Owen so that I would get some sort of understanding of the reality of war. Owen wrote from personal experience and was really into what he called "the horror of war." The best poem was one called "Dulce et Decorum Est" and it's about a group of very exhausted and part-wounded English soldiers returning from the front line trenches for a bit of a rest when they are hit by a gas attack. One of the soldiers can't get his mask on in time and dies a painful death in front of the others, who aren't able to help him. The teacher asked me what I thought was the main point of the poem and got a bit worked up when I said that the main point was either about the inadequacy of army training or the inadequacy of the equipment, because even though the soldier was exhausted, and possibly wounded, he should have been able to get his mask on in time. I said the equipment was probably fine, so it was a good job that he was the one to die because he was the obvious weak link in the platoon and the group was better off without him. The teacher said I was completely missing the point and that the poem is all about the horrors and brutality of war, but I said that it was he who was completely missing the point. What the hell do people like him think war is going to be like? It is supposed to be brutal and ugly and disgusting. That is why it is called war. And I know I would love every brutal, ugly and disgusting second. Trust me, I would.

As you know, I am a big-time Rommel fan and one day I might admit him to my team—have to do a lot more thinking about that, though. I suppose I could have a reserve bench of high-impact players, like in rugby. I could have Rommel, Jesus Christ and Mr. Wihongi—and who knows, I may even sneak in Joan of Arc, because I'm definitely not sexist, but I won't have her harping on about visitations from saints. No way!

# 101

# CHAPTER SEVEN

Monday morning's staff meeting had started and Terry's seat was empty as usual. The talk had once again turned to Hamish and once again they were getting nowhere. An energy-sapping fog seemed to engulf the staff whenever they discussed Hamish these days. Sarah Quinn took advantage of a heavy lull in the discussion.

"But surely all this talk of death and killing is some sort of cry for help?"

"Do you actually believe that nonsense, Sarah?" Simon hissed, bristling at the thought. "The boy has a death obsession because he is mentally ill. He is a delusional sociopath and the time has come for us to admit that we are not running a holding pen for the mentally ill. We simply can't provide Hamish with the help he needs. Let's pretend that we are in charge here and remove him, before the courts force us to and we all look like total fools."

"Oh fine, let's just wash our hands of him, then, make him someone else's problem, like other places have done all his life so far!" Sarah replied.

"So it's okay for him to have a free run of the place, is it?" Simon asked. "How the hell is he able to break into our computer system at will? I've had to change my password three times this week, but no, we can't do anything about that because little Hamish must have his computer so he can write his precious journal. And what a load of pretentious bloody twaddle that's turning out to be. I've had enough!"

Sarah was about to reply when Helen finally pulled herself from the fog.

"Stop it, both of you! Unfortunately, I think Simon's right, and you can stop looking at me like that, Sarah, and you too, Toko—it's not an admission of defeat. One side of me does want to hold on to him. In some ways he has quite a positive impact on the other boys. Since he's become deputy top dog, minor scraps have almost ceased. He seems to have some sort of odd calming effect on the boys. Sure, at first he had as little to do with them as possible, but have you noticed him engaging a lot more with them lately? On the other hand, I admit that he is utterly unpredictable. Toko, you eventually told me yourself that if you hadn't blocked the taiaha blow, it might well have cracked Victor Kaiarahi's head wide open! Sorry, but I'm afraid he has to go."

Almost on cue, Terry walked in and announced, "He's saved you the trouble, folks. Matron's just told me his bed was empty this morning. She was holding back from telling you until she was certain he wasn't playing silly buggers somewhere, but he's definitely gone."

"What? Gone where?" Helen demanded.

"Who knows? None of the boys saw him go. Matron's already rung the police. He did leave this note, though. Don't snatch, Simon, I'll read it. Right then, here we go. Gosh, he appears to have left certain people off the greeting."

"Just read the bloody thing, please, Terry!" Helen said.

"Okay, okay!"

Dear Terry and Mr. Wihongi. By the time you are all reading this note, I'll be long gone—ha, that sounds a bit like a country-and-western line, eh, Terry? I knew that it was only a matter of time before Grenville and Whittle decided to call in the men in white coats to haul crazy old Hamish off to some bad boy nuthouse, so I thought I'd save them the trouble. I'm tired of being treated like a freak show kid and think it is best for everyone if I do the honorable thing. Terry—you are the only caseworker who ever took me seriously. Our talks were very cool, or should I say cerebral (that's word thirty-seven on our list). Just get rid of the piercings and don't get any more idiotic tattoos. They make you look stupid and you're not.

Mr. Wihongi, you're the man! And you don't need to worry—I won't tell anyone why you had to leave the army. I found out last week by hacking into a defense forces database and making two phone calls. Army security is a joke and it's just as well that lately we've been a fairly lame country that stays out of scraps. You did your best and shouldn't feel bad because those guys with you couldn't follow orders and gave up. They just weren't up to it and the army has to find those sorts of things out. How would they have coped in a firefight situation? They wouldn't have, so I reckon you did the army a favor by weeding them out.

I wouldn't have let you down. I would love to

have been up there with you. In my dreams now there are five of us—Alexander the Great, Charles Upham, Te Rauparaha, you and me—up against the rest of the world! But anyway, I'm glad you survived that day. It just wasn't your time to die either. Once I said that you are wasted here, but now I know why you came. I think you feel guilty and ashamed about what happened, but you don't have to. Look at all the lives you're saving now. And yeah, I know about you and Victor, and I reckon you owe it to him to tell him why you're here. He will probably be upset, but still, he isn't a kid anymore and has the right to know. Terry, can you tell Victor and Noel this next stuff?

Terry looked up from the page. "Well, I don't know if I should read this part out."

"Read it, Terry!" Helen snapped.

Terry continued.

Victor—sorry for stabbing you with the fork and trying to waste you with the taiaha. Nothing personal. You are okay and I think you can do whatever you want with your life because you're smart and people look up to you, even the staff.

You don't need to be a loser gangsta, just be Victor. I am leaving you all my books—don't laugh, I reckon you will enjoy them. There are two very cool ones about Te Rauparaha and you can learn heaps from him, believe me! The other boys don't need to know. On second thoughts, let them know. Let them know who you really are. Oh yeah, Mr. Wihongi will probably come and tell you some important information. I want you to handle it. It wasn't his fault.

Hey, Noel—don't let anyone push you around. Not the staff or the boys. Just take your own good time with speaking, and when you get to go home, make sure you keep up the rapping. Ever thought of getting into some sort of DJ work? Do a course at a local polytechnic. Go for it, man!

So anyway, this is crazy Hamish signing off. Thanks again, Terry and Mr. Wihongi—yeah, and you others. You do a good job most of the time, even if you are too soft on the boys. I have written a letter to my parents. It's in my top drawer. Terry, can you post it? It's my time, Hamish Graham.

P.S. I have decided to write a diary of my "travels," a bit like Scott of the Antarctic, because I know how much you have enjoyed my journal writing—especially you, Mr. Whittle! Wouldn't want you to have to go cold turkey on me, eh. So I guess if you find me, you will find my diary as well. Isn't that something to look forward to?

"And that's it," Terry said quietly.

Helen slumped in her chair. "Oh God, he could be anywhere. Do you think he's gone back to Wellington? How is he traveling? What will he do? Do 'it's my time' and 'like Scott of the Antarctic' mean what I think they mean?"

"Helen, calm down!" Simon said. "The police will be here soon and they'll know exactly what to do. He's probably headed into the central city, don't you think? That's where a fourteen-year-old kid would gravitate to, surely?"

Instant counter-theories from Terry and Sarah suggested Hamish was holed up somewhere in the near vicinity, watching their reactions, hiding up a tree in the nearest thick bush or heading for a West Coast beach.

Toko read the letter again quietly, then announced, "No, I know where he's going—Waiouru. He will attempt to climb the eastern side of Mount Ruapehu and scale a certain peak. I know the exact area."

In the time it took the police to arrive, Toko had explained how he knew where Hamish was going. He took a long time to begin.

"This is very difficult for me, but I think I need to tell you what Hamish appears to have already found out. As you know, before coming here I was a physical training instructor in the army. Part of my job was breaking in the recruits, toughening them up and trying to instill the discipline they would need to survive army life. Anyway, a couple of years ago we had a particularly troublesome new bunch. Several had gang backgrounds and thought they would easily handle army life, but like a lot of the new ones, they were soft as jelly underneath all the bullshit. If I had my way, we would never take these guys on; they're more trouble than they're worth.

"I decided to take six of the more difficult recruits, all with gang backgrounds, on an early winter tramp up the eastern slopes of Mount Ruapehu. You know, do survival training and team skills in an environment that leaves no room for stuff ups. Don't know how familiar you are with the area, but about twenty kilometers north of Waiouru, on the main highway, you come to the Whangaehu River, which feeds directly off the mountain. We followed the river straight west to the foothills and then headed directly up to the mountain trail, ending up at the Rangipo

Hut late that afternoon. We did a few snow drills before settling in for the night. In hindsight I was probably a bit annoyed that they had all handled this first day pretty well, so I decided to push them really hard the next day and see how high I could get them up Girdlestone Peak. It's about 2,600 meters above sea level and would be a genuine challenge for the guys.

"The weather was okay when we left early next morning for the tramp to the base of the peak, but the snow was really thick and the going was tough. We took three hours just to get to the base—then all hell let loose. A predicted southerly change hit almost a full day before expected, and within fifteen minutes we had driving wind and sleet with visibility reducing fast. No, that's not quite true. I knew that a southerly was coming, maybe not quite that soon, though. I should have turned back immediately and headed straight for the hut, but I didn't. I thought, Good, this will sort them out—this will show them how tough they really are. I radioed our position and we dug out a large snow cave at the base of a cliff face beside the Wahianoa Glacier. We got into our survival clothing, squeezed into the cave and settled in to wait out the storm, which I thought would blow over in a couple of hours. But no such luck. It went on all that night, getting progressively worse, and things looked no better at first light. It was seriously cold and during the night we lost radio contact with base. Here is where I made my second mistake. Instead of cutting my losses and heading directly for the hut, I decided to move us to a new location, slightly higher but more in the lee of the cliff face. The guys were scared and tired but appeared to be still operating reasonably well. A couple of them were all for striking out for the hut, but I told them that in the conditions, it was far too dangerous. I laid down the law and said we just had to tough it out. I roped us together for the hundred-meter haul to our new snow cave site and we set off. Halfway there, the boy immediately behind me yanked the rope and yelled to me that the last two were gone. Apparently they just untied themselves and decided to head back to the hut. I dug the others into a makeshift snow cave, threatened them with God knows what if they moved one inch and then set off to try and find the other two. I found them an hour later. They had walked off the trail and fallen into a deep crevasse. I managed to climb down to them to find one dead and the other as good as dead. I held the boy in my arms while he died. He was only nineteen.

"There was an army inquiry and it was found that I was negligent but given the extenuating circumstances, I could not be held responsible for the boys' deaths. I disagreed. My stubbornness and arrogance killed those boys. It was all about how tough I was and how weak they were in comparison. It was also me letting my hatred of gangs get the better of me. Despite the top brass's protests, I resigned immediately and soon after ended up here. It wasn't a random decision, though. The boy who died in my arms was Victor Kaiarahi's brother, Charlie. God knows how, but Hamish seems to have found this out. It was clear to me that Charlie had massive internal injuries and was dying, so I tried to comfort him in his last moments. We talked about his whanau and he told me of his younger brother, who had been the star of the family but was now in an institution called New Horizons Boys' Home. Charlie made me promise I would look after his younger brother, who he said was a good kid, not a bastard like him. And then he died. A promise made to a dying man has to be kept—I had no choice. And Hamish is right about another thing too. I have to tell Victor the truth about how his brother died. He deserves to know that I am responsible for his older brother's death."

Toko's story had eaten up all the air. There was a deep silence in the room. Helen cleared her throat. "I see . . . and so you think that Hamish will try and get to Waiouru?"

"I know it's where he's gone. Tomorrow is the anniversary of the boys' deaths, and my guess is that Hamish will attempt to climb Girdlestone Peak, as some sort of ultimate challenge—and unless I find him first, he will die in the process. But first I'm going to tell Victor the truth about why I came here."

**101**
**PART**
**TWO** *Departure*

# 101
# CHAPTER
# ONE

The six boys in C Dorm were sleeping like babies. All except one. Hamish noted, and not for the first time, that at a certain time in the night, usually about two o'clock, his five roommates somehow managed to synchronize their breathing. He recalled reading somewhere that this was not uncommon with soldiers, who after months or even years of sleeping together in cramped, close quarters would adjust their sleeping patterns and operate as one sleeping body. He was about to file these thoughts away under "must think more about this and work out the physiological reasons," when he remembered his plan and the dead end it probably involved.

He quietly slipped out of bed, already fully dressed,

and went through the contents of his day pack—water, flashlight, matches, knife, rope, muesli bars, map and compass. The only concessions he made to the chilly early winter conditions were to include a thermal top, a polar fleece jacket, wool gloves and socks and a pair of sturdy boots he'd found in the tractor shed. But for the first part of the journey he was dressed in tidy, dark-colored casuals—nothing that would draw attention. Hamish's last act before leaving was to take out a new, hard-covered notebook. He sat on his bed and started to write in quick and surprisingly tidy longhand.

### Diary Entry 1—July 31, 2:15 a.m.

I suppose diary writing is a bit different from journal writing, but I'm not sure in what way. Well, obviously a lot more personal. I'm certainly not going to start each entry with "Dear Diary"—how lame would that be? This diary will be a serious and exact record of what happens between now and when I am found. I was going to say "if I am found," but that wouldn't make sense because if I am not found, then no one could be reading this diary, and that would be stupid. My diary-writing hero has to be the Englishman Sir Robert Falcon Scott. What a man—and what a cool name! He and three tough companions set out in 1910 to be the first men to reach the South Pole, but when they finally arrived in January 1912, they discovered that this rugged-as Norwegian guy called Roald Amundsen had beaten them by a month. What a major bummer! On the way back to their base hut they got hit by really bad weather and suffered from various illnesses and, to cut a long (but great) story short, they all died. But old Scott wrote right up to when he died of cold and starvation, and everything he wrote made sense—not some "woe is me" rambling bullshit. So that's what this will be like— the sense bit, I mean.

Anyway, I am sitting on my bed just about to leave this "secure facility." Why do they bother calling it secure when it so obviously isn't? A retarded and partially blind five-year-old could escape from here. For a start the alarm system is a joke! You can't have the wiring of a serious alarm system exposed for any idiot to see. It needs to be internalized so that it can't be disabled, and you also need to upgrade to a sensor-type system that trips on movement or light beams being broken. Of course, if you want to get really serious about preventing escapes at night, you need to get a couple of half-starved attack dogs. Mind you, that would never be allowed in this enlightened age because someone might get hurt! I would actually feel better right now if

I had to earn this escape by outwitting ultra-tough security. Man, I would love to have been with Upham during one of his escapes. What a blast, knowing that if you get caught, you would be tortured or killed. As you might guess, I am a bit of an escape fan. Our best peacetime escape artist (that's what they are) was a guy called George Wilder in the 1960s, who escaped from every prison they put him in. He became a kind of folk hero and even had a song written about him.

I said this was a serious diary, so I have to stop getting sidetracked, which unfortunately I do quite a lot when I'm writing about major interesting topics like escaping or any of my heroes. Right, so now I am about to walk out and start my little adventure. I have that shit-hot nervous feeling you get before doing something ultra-dangerous. You know, your senses get very sharp and things kind of slow down around you—very cool. If you don't know what I'm talking about, then you have never done anything really dangerous and are probably a sad loser like most people these days. And before you get all stroppy, I don't mean safe stuff like bungee jumping or going on a roller coaster. That's just exciting, not dangerous. I mean stuff like balancing on the twenty-centimeter-wide window ledge of a thirty-story building, where one mistake means near certain death, or breaking into the house of ultra-tough dudes when you know they are sleeping inside.

I once broke into a neighbor's house at night (not the losers with the dogs) just for the thrill of it. They had just installed a fancy security system that I figured would trip an alarm if you tried to force any doors or main windows or if you walked through any parts of the house near the front and back doors and so, as you can imagine, I just had to have a go at cracking the system. I planned it like a military operation: black shirt and track pants, black shoe polish on my face and thin black gloves, because no way does someone with my record want to leave prints. Like a lot of people, they always left a small upper window open in the toilet and so that's where I decided to get in. As you know, I'm quite skinny and climbing up the outside piping and squeezing through this little window proved child's play for a pro like me. I didn't want to steal anything, so I just sat in the lounge for a while and listened to the night noises of a strange house—very cool! The best part was when the man of the house got up to go to the loo. He had to walk right past where I was sitting in the lounge, and if he'd looked in, he might have seen me. He is a real serious dude, you know, very proper and all, so I almost exploded when he let rip with this huge fart while he was taking a leak. Anyway, all this was a major buzz because the guy didn't like me much (understatement) and would have been fairly upset that I was sitting in his lounge at three o'clock in the morning, the day after he had spent megabucks on a fancy security system. I had to do something to piss him off, though, so before I left, I decided to rearrange the lounge furniture. This took ages because I had to be utterly silent and their furniture was kind of old-fashioned and heavy as hell. The home theater system had about a thousand cords to unplug and set up again, and I was operating in virtual darkness! Once I had it set up, I had to do a quick check to ensure I had it operating correctly, on mute of course, because I couldn't have them thinking they had been hit by a technically stupid home invader. They should have been grateful to me really, because the idiot had the speakers attached incorrectly. The funniest thing I did was to flip all the paintings and photos over. Man, I would love to have seen the fat jerk's face when he got up in the morning. I was the main suspect, of course, but they couldn't pin anything on me, and as nothing was taken, the cops weren't too interested in doing anything. Sorry, all this was a major sidetrack—but who cares? Diary writing is for me, not for others, so if I want to get sidetracked, I just will! How will I end each diary entry? I think I'll just write my name.

Hamish

Leaving the home itself was a piece of cake for Hamish. There was an alarm system he had silenced earlier that night, and after fifteen minutes of diary writing he was heading southwest at a light trot, aiming for State Highway 1. It was cold, with a niggling southerly breeze, but Hamish was very fit and capable of keeping up this slow-but-steady pace for hours.

Shortly after three o'clock he stopped at a road that linked with the main highway south and crawled into a patch of scrubby bush to eat a muesli bar and plan his next move. For Hamish's plan to work, he needed to be at Waiouru by at least ten in the morning—less than seven hours away. He decided that he couldn't risk public transport, and it was likely to be too slow anyway, and instead he would hitch a lift. He looked considerably older than his fourteen years, but anyone hitching a lift at this time in the morning was going to be regarded suspiciously. Wanting to be dropped off in Waiouru on a winter morning, and with a weather forecast promising squally showers and possibly snow, while not cause for suspicion could be seen as a bit odd. Hamish decided to worry about this problem when he needed to and concentrate his energies on securing a lift with the right sort of person—someone who wanted company and wouldn't ask too many questions.

He was no stranger to hitching and regarded it as something of a science. Make eye contact, give a confident smile, wear tidy clothes, carry only one bag and allow plenty of pull-in space. Yes, Hamish knew all the tricks. But this was different. It was just after three o'clock on a cold, dark Friday morning, and unfortunately he couldn't risk hitching on the motorway itself. It had to be this more isolated connecting road. He decided to walk as close as he could to the motorway on-ramp and see who turned up.

Hamish was having a quick drink from his water bottle but froze when he heard rapidly approaching footsteps.

"Oi, what are ya doin' hiding in there?" a voice from the dark called.

Hamish remained utterly silent.

"I seen ya running past my shed back up the road, so stop muckin' about and come out where I can see ya. Come on, let's be havin' ya!"

There was nothing for it but to come out and face whoever this was. If he couldn't bluff his way out of it, he would just take off. He crawled out of the scrub and looked up at his discoverer. A heavily built Pakeha man of about fifty, wearing gum boots, stubbies shorts and a black sleeveless undershirt, stared down at Hamish. The man's muscular arms and chest were covered in elaborate tattoos. Hamish slowly stood up and took stock of the stranger. He remained silent.

"Huh. A kid. How old are you, boy—fifteen or sixteen? Yeah, well, I seen ya hoofing it down the road past me shed, and I thinks to myself, now there's a fella in a hurry, wonder what he's stolen or whose wife he's just shagged? So, which is it, kid?"

"My name's not kid, it's Andrew, and I haven't done anything. I'm just going for a bit of a run."

"Yeah, well, I can see that, boy, but where to and why? Had some prick break into me shed last week and pinch me best fuckin' socket set, so that's why I'm askin', see! Nah—I can see you're not the sort to pinch tools."

The man stepped back to get a better look at Hamish.

"I'll tell you who I think you are and what you're doin', eh? I reckon you're one of the kids from that New Horizons Boys' Home and you're doin' a runner. Yeah, I'm right, eh? Even in this light I can see by your eyes. You have to be sharp to beat old Trev Mitchell." He thrust out a large paw. "Yeah, well, that's who I am, so who are you?

And don't tell me Andrew or I'll clip ya ear. I can always tell when people are lyin' to me, see."

The big man's handshake was firm and held no malice. Hamish decided he needed to play his next few moves dead straight.

"I'm Hamish Graham and yes, I am running away from the New Horizons Boys' Home. I'm trying to hitch a lift to Waiouru and I need to be there by about ten."

"The New Horizons Boys' Home—what a bloody mouthful. Called them borstals in my day, mate, and I should know. Spent half my youth in the fuckers. Here's what's gunna happen, okay—you're gunna come back to my place, back up the road, have some tucker with me, and then we're gunna hit the road. This is your lucky day, matey! Reason I'm up so early is to be on the road by four. I'm taking me new hot rod down to Upper Hutt for a meet. I'll have ya in Waiouru before you can say 'Fuck the lot of them.' We can trade notes on borstal ex-periences. Come on, Hamish, I need a cup of tea and a fag and you're gunna have a decent feed before goin' anywhere with me. Jeez, you're a scrawny bugger, don't they feed you proper in that place?"

Trev lived in a large and very well-appointed caravan parked behind an implement shed filled with a chaotic jumble of tools and car parts. Pride of place was reserved for a bright red 1964 Chevrolet truck and a homemade hot rod dragster, which was perched on a double tandem trailer attached to the truck. Despite Hamish's protests, Trev fixed him a breakfast of eggs, bacon, hash browns and toast, all of which disappeared in a short time.

"See, told ya you was hungry. Can't fool old Trev, matey! So how come a tidy-looking young bloke like you is coolin' ya heels in borstal?"

"I do violent things," Hamish said, expecting a mocking response.

"Violent things, eh? Hmm, yeah, I suppose you might nut off occasionally, mate, there's something a bit odd about your eyes. Eyes are the windows to the soul, did you know that, kid? Aha! See? I called you 'kid' on purpose then and your eyes flashed like when I called you kid before—and you have a really low blink rate. I bet none of the shrinks at that New Horizons place even know that, eh? Low blink rate means you can concentrate and think. I came across a few blokes like you in my borstal days. Kids from good families usually, bright as all fuck, but square pegs in round holes. Came across quite a few young blokes like that on the oil rigs too. Most of them were frustrated and angry little buggers. Know how I'd fix you? I'd turn you loose on whatever turns you on. Just tell you to go for it."

Hamish was astonished. Trev knew more about him in five minutes than most of his therapists had learned in the last five years, but he concealed his admiration with a question of his own.

"So what turned you on, then?" Hamish asked.

"Good one, matey, always play ya cards close to ya chest. Well, I'll tell ya, then. Mechanics turned me on. An old warder in Invercargill Borstal sussed this out when I helped him fix up his old Matchless 500 motorbike. He got me into fixing up things, like stuffed lawn mowers and old tractors. I reckon the old bugger saved my life because he found me a diesel mechanic's apprenticeship with a mate of his when I got out and I've been in work ever since—all over the world too, matey, but mostly on oil rigs in the North Sea. I returned to New Zealand three years ago, rich as fuck, not like most of the *drongos* on the rigs who piss it all up whenever they're on leave. Come on, matey, take that last bit of toast with you, we're off. I'll bore you shitless all the way."

# CHAPTER
## TWO

"Okay, matey? Comfy? Don't doze off on me, eh—I need
ya to roll fags. Yeah, well, like I said, I'll tell ya about me,
then it can be your turn, and before ya know it, we'll be
in Waiouru. Everyone thought I was dumb. My mother,
my father—especially my father—and every teacher I
ever had. I didn't get the hang of reading until I was
about ten or eleven and I'm still pretty hopeless at writing. Don't look at me like that, matey. Today they've got
labels for guys like me, labels like dyslexic and hyperac-
tive, and I read somewhere that some schools even have
teacher aides to sit with these kids and help them learn.
When I was a kid, the labels I got were stupid, lazy and

bad, and the only aides the teachers ever used with me were the strap and the cane.

"When I think back, my childhood seemed to be one long fight—fights with me father, fights with me brothers, fights with me teachers—I dunno, fights with just about everyone. I had this long-running scrap with a kid called Gerard at the Catholic primary school I went to in Invercargill. We were the biggest kids in Form Two—you guys have another name for it now; we were twelve years old. All the other kids would egg us on, encourage us to fight, so we would. If they were bored, one of them would just have to yell out 'Scrap!' and within a minute or two me an' Gerard would be slugging it out. Eventually one of the brothers would wade in with cane swinging to break it up and then give us a few more whacks once we'd stopped. The weird thing is that me and Gerard were mates really and would often walk home together, comparing cuts and bruises on the way. It pisses me off mightily that I allowed the other little shits to use us like that. Wonder what ever happened to old Gerard? Last time I saw him he was talking about headin' to Oz to work in the mines out west.

"Man, we had some right crazy teachers, though. The brothers were the worst. I think they had this sort of inferiority complex about not being as high up the God ladder as priests. There was this one crazy bugger who called his bamboo cane 'William' and would hold long conversations with it. 'William' was kept in a special cupboard at the back of the room and when this brother was bored or frustrated and felt like caning someone, he would pretend that the cane was calling to him. His current little favorite pupil would be told, 'Go and fetch my little friend William—he might be lonely in that dark old cupboard and want to talk to someone.' He'd then hold the cane to his ear and say, 'What's that, William? You *are* lonely? You *do* want to talk to someone? Well, we can't have poor old William feeling lonely, now, can we, boys? I wonder who it is that William wants to talk to?' He'd then do this sick, sadistic routine, working his way through various kids' names, all of whom were hoping like hell it would be some other kid and not them who was about to get the crap belted out of him. 'Now who is it you want to talk to, William? Is it O'Connell? No? Are you sure now, William, because his handwriting is getting awful messy lately. No? Well, maybe if his writing doesn't improve, you can talk to him another time soon. Now, let me see. Ahh . . . I know who it must be, then. It's Simpson, isn't it? Yes, that's right, it has to be Simpson because I definitely heard him use disgusting gutter language outside the bike sheds this morning, William. You know, the sort of language the state school children like to use all the time, and we all know how much you hate to hear the Lord's good name used in vain. What? It's not him? Come on now, William, this isn't like you. You must be getting soft in your old age! He's getting soft, isn't he, boys?' At this point we would all agree nervously, knowing the game was nearing its grisly conclusion.

"Hey, you think I'm pulling ya leg, don't ya, matey? I'm not—this is straight up. Eventually the prick would tire of the routine and say something like, 'Now, William, if you don't tell me, I'll have to snap you in half and get myself another cane. What do you say, boys? Shall I just snap old William in half? What do you say, O'Leary? Shall I just snap old William in half? Shut up, boy, William's talking to me now. Ah yes, William, I thought you would eventually tell me. Well, come on, then, the boys and I are waiting to hear. Who is it, then? No, no, it can't be! Are you sure now, William? But he's such a good boy. Collins, you say? What did Michael Collins do, William? He what? I don't believe you! He cheated in the spelling test! Are you trying to tell me that Collins was too lazy to learn his words and had to lower himself to cheating in the spelling test? Now, William, let's be sure about this. Are you honestly telling me that Collins, who used to be such a good boy, would let himself, his entire family, his teachers and his classmates down by cheating in our weekly spelling test?' At which point poor Collins, or whoever, would be dragged to the front and have two or three vicious strokes across the hand with a bloody big bamboo cane—unless it was me being caned, when it would be five or six strokes. And that bloody thing hurt, mate, every time.

"Usually you would know when your turn was coming. Once I really pissed him off by standing up and marching to the front of the room, hand extended and spoiling his fun. 'William wants to speak to me, so stop the crap and get on with it!' Man, did I get the snot beaten out of me! But do you know what, matey? I never once gave the prick the satisfaction of seeing me cry, or even flinch. I would stare him in the eye every time and say something smart like, 'Thank you, Brother, I needed that.'

"One day, toward the end of Form Two, I'd had enough of the shit and refused to be caned. I just couldn't be bothered with it anymore and said, 'Cane me again and I'll stick William up your fat arse.' The boys were stunned and the teacher made a lunge for me, but even though I had just turned thirteen, I was nearly as big as he was, and he pulled up real quick when I held my ground, fists raised. Then I just walked out and thus ended my formal education.

"Dad had run off by then, and Mum couldn't do much with me, so I just mucked about at home or hung around town getting into trouble. My oldest brother was an apprentice mechanic and sometimes his boss would let me stay there for an afternoon helping out with odd jobs for a few shillings. To everyone's surprise, mine included, I took to motors real easy—learned to drive too. There's sort of a logic to engines that I found addictive and I'd spend hours round the back of the workshop so I wouldn't get in the boss's way, taking apart and reassembling old motors. It became an obsession with me and I started quietly nickin' tools so I could start up my own little garage at home.

"This might have gone on for some time without anyone being any the wiser, but one day when the guys were all at smoko, I went too far and decided to take this beautiful 1958 Citroën they'd been workin' on for a quick test drive. You know the car I mean? Beautiful flowing curves, a real female car, if you know what I mean. I discovered that the timing was still way out so I took it back to my workshop at home for some tappet adjustments. When I returned two hours later, the boss went apeshit. No one guessed that it was me who had taken it, and the cops were on the lookout for a major car thief. He calmed down a tiny bit when I told him I had it humming beautifully, but I definitely wasn't welcome there anymore.

"By now I was hooked—I needed my daily dose of car oil, and the only way I could get my fix was to start pinching cars for real. Back then, nickin' cars was a lot easier than it is now. People were pretty trusting on the whole, and heaps of people wouldn't even bother removing the keys from the ignition when they stopped to go to the shops or something. Some silly buggers would even leave the engine running if they were only stopping for a little while. Unfortunately I helped to change those habits by 'borrowing' cars for joyrides. I had a rule I stuck to, though—I would always do a little job on the car before I returned it, even if it was just cleaning the plugs or giving it a quick wash back at my workshop. Sometimes I would leave a note to the owner saying things like, 'Hey, you need to change the oil!' or 'Your fan belt is gunna break!'

"Eventually I was caught, of course, but the cops went easy on me, especially after the local paper and radio station made out I was like some kind of thirteen-year-old Robin Hood. All I got was a suspended sentence and a warning.

"The next time I pinched a car, I just kept going until

I ran out of gas. I ended up in a little town called Pleasant Point, inland from Timaru. I had a few bob saved and hung out for a couple of days, parked down by a river. Eventually I ran out of food and walked back into the town. I went to the local garage and said I was looking for a few days' work. The owner was a good bloke called Tom, and after I passed a quick test adjusting the timing on a Vauxhall, he took me on for a week helpin' to clear a backlog of work on all these school buses he used to run. He said I could doss down in an old cottage behind the garage. I couldn't stay there forever, though, and eventually I had to tell Tom what I had done. He said he had to call the cops, but he still paid me for the week and even gave me a ten-quid bonus, a hell of a lot in those days.

"This time I was put into a boys' home for kids too young to go to borstal, but I'm not going to tell you anything about that place—all I'll say is that the boss there made that crazy teacher I told you about seem like Mahatma Gandhi. I came out of there twice as tough and bad as when I went in.

"I kept getting in and out of trouble for the next couple of years, but then I had the best break a boy like me could have. I got done for breaking and entry (to a garage, of course) and got sent for a twelve-month stretch to Invercargill Borstal. You probably think I'm gunna tell you bad stuff about the place, eh? No way, mate! I really liked it there. I had one big fight when I first started, just to let the guys know that I wasn't to be messed with, and then I just got on with it. The food was the best I had ever had in my life—three meals a day with heaps of meat and spuds, and we had regular lessons in woodwork, metalwork and even practical math. We had a good rugby team too, and during the time I was there, we won the Invercargill Under-Nineteen Division. But best of all I got to meet old Cyril.

"Cyril was this hard-as-nails old Pommy warder who took us brighter boys for a sort of practical engineering course. His word was law in the workshop, and even though he must have been about seventy, if you mucked about, he would take you out the back and kick you real hard in the arse with his big hobnail boots. He had a very neat little scam going where he would advertise himself in the local paper as a handyman who would fix up lawn mowers, chain saws, washing machines—in fact, anything with a motor in it and small enough for him to fit in his old van. He'd then bring them to us boys and we'd fix them. He shared the profits with us too, so it was the perfect scam. The borstal bosses must have known about it, but because it kept everyone happy, they kept quiet. I was the best at fixing motors, and since me and Cyril got on real well, he said he would arrange for me to get into a diesel mechanic apprenticeship with a mate of his when I was released. So you can see that borstal saved my life—never looked back since!"

# CHAPTER THREE

Shortly before ten o'clock Trev pulled to a stop outside the Waiouru Army Museum. He turned the engine off and stared hard at Hamish. "I don't know what it is, but I know you're up to something. I'm not happy about droppin' you here, matey, but hey, I'm not your bloody father, am I? Tell you what, though, I'm giving you my cell phone number, and if you don't call me by six o'clock tonight, I'm calling the coppers."

"Fair enough, Trev. Thanks for the lift, and you didn't bore me shitless." Hamish wanted to say lots more, but his eyes suddenly brimmed with tears and he turned away in hot embarrassment and shock.

"Yeah, you're a good kid. Make sure you look me up, eh? You can tell me more about Alexander the Great and I'll tell you more about oil rigs. Here's my number; now bugger off and stop blubbin'—shit, you'll be startin' me soon."

With a throaty V-8 roar, the truck powered off into the stiff southerly wind, leaving Hamish all alone. He shouldered his pack and walked toward the museum.

## Diary Entry 2—July 31, 10:30 a.m.

I am sitting behind the museum, where I have been farewelling Charles Upham. Luckily, I was the only visitor in the museum, so I could spend some real quality time in Valour Alcove, just sort of breathing in the life force of the medals, especially Upham's VCs. Some people get off on cemeteries remembering important people, but I don't know, they just seem empty places to me. I reckon if you want to remember someone, you have to go to a place that meant a lot to the person or be in the presence of a really major personal item, like these medals. I like that Maori word *taonga*—to me these medals are treasures of the highest order. The first time I came here with Dad, I was kind of overcome with the atmosphere of the place. I mean, everything is just so awesome. It's like the designers made a place just for me. The building itself is tough and gray and harsh-looking, and I love the way it just sort of squats in the tussock.

That first time we were returning from a mind-numbingly dull trip visiting Dad's mother in Hamilton for her 140th or something birthday. Old Gran was always full of really thoughtful advice for how I should be dealt with! She usually began these tirades (good word, thanks, Terry) with, "Of course, Morris, you've always been far too soft with him." The next bit of the script was inevitably, "In my day we were taught to respect our elders, and watch out if you didn't!" and on bad days she would launch into insomnia-curing stories of her upbringing on a dairy farm near Te Awamutu. Even if I was right there beside her, she always spoke about me as if I was invisible. Yeah, me and Gran didn't really hit it off, but I suppose she wasn't a bad old bird in some ways, and some of her farming stories weren't too bad. Anyway, I pestered them to stop at the museum. Mum was not happy about this at all, as she and some brain-dead child psychologist had this big thing going about trying to get me away from my so-called obsession with military matters. Like that's really going to work! I used to wind this guy up by saying crazy things like how I had this uncontrollable urge to shoot up my school. He would show me various images and pictures and I had to say the first thing that came into my mind. Whatever the dumb image was, I would say something like "torture" or "genocide" just to point out to him how pathetic and childish this brilliant psychoanalysis technique was. In the end I told him that I was just having him on and he said, "Yes, I know. But they are still the associations that first come into your mind, and I don't know about you, but I find that very interesting." The next time we did it, I changed everything to associations like "fluffy bunny rabbits" and "smiling angels." He kind of got the point then, I think. Anyway, I said that if they didn't stop at the museum, I would open the car door and simply throw myself out and they would have to live with my death for the rest of their miserable lives. So they stopped, and of course, I loved every single thing about the museum. Imagine when I discovered the Valour Alcove and saw Charles Upham's medals. I stood there for ages and Mum went a bit loopy because she said that I went into some kind of nonresponsive trance, but I was only doing that heroes game I make up sometimes. I think, in that one, Upham and I were charging at a row of German panzers, leaping over fallen comrades, tommy guns blazing and screaming bloodcurdling oaths. I can sometimes get so into those games that you could stick pins in me and I wouldn't even feel them.

I couldn't stay as long as I would have liked just now because I have to get my challenge under way, and I didn't want to get into a lovefest with the staff. As you can imagine, they don't get too many teenagers like me there, and I seem to have become their pet pinup boy. If you want to see my charming face, you only have to look at their latest brochure.

Okay, I am now going to head north back up the highway, but I'll stay off the road to avoid being seen. I'm going to try and reach a trail I saw on the way here that leads to the Tukino ski field. I can follow that for a bit, then head southwest toward the foothills of the mountain. I am feeling a bit weird at the moment. A strange mix of excitement and a new feeling that could be fear, or maybe doubt. I don't think I have ever felt scared about anything in my life, so I don't really know how to react to this feeling. Doubt or uncertainty are also new feelings for me. I hate weak people and always just plow straight ahead with whatever I'm doing, but yeah . . . all I know is that I feel ultra-nervous but kind of edgy, like in a horror movie when the camera zeros right in on the subject and the high-pitched music tells you that the sicko with the carving knife is just around the corner. I will have to jog all the way there and it will take me about an hour. If all goes well, I will write my next entry in a shelter I saw on my map called the Rangipo Hut. And that's kind of fitting because I think there's a prison with the same name somewhere near Turangi. Maybe the prison service has these special huts set up around the place so prisoners on the run can have somewhere to stay while being hunted down.

Hamish

Covering ground off-road was easier said than done, and an hour later, Hamish was still several kilometers short of the Tukino trail. He checked north and south for vehicles, then quickly crossed the road. Hamish pulled his jacket collar up to give more protection against the biting wind and dropped down onto the banks of what he thought had to be the Whangaehu River. As he contemplated the alien landscape of the Desert Road, the enormity of what he was doing suddenly hit him and he was forced to take several slow, deep breaths. When he had mastered his panic, he sat on the spongy ground to pull on his hiking gear and consult the map once more.

Hamish knew that time was in short supply. He was fairly certain Mr. Wihongi would work out where he was going and would probably organize some sort of rescue attempt. What was less certain was why he had laid out such obvious clues in his letter. Hadn't Mr. Wihongi already suffered enough on these slopes? Before writing the letter, he had thought Mr. Wihongi would understand, and maybe even approve of, his final act. Toko finding him on the top of Girdlestone Peak, holding him close at the end. But now, with the cloud-shrouded mountain looming ahead, his plan seemed childish and pathetic. Toko's arm was still in a cast and he would surely leave any rescue attempt to the police or the army. Well, to hell with them all, no turning back now, Hamish thought.

The distance was deceptive and after an hour Hamish was still less than halfway to the foothills of the mountain. He was certain the police would use tracker dogs, and his rock-hopping and periodic doubling back to confuse the dogs had eaten up valuable time. The labored thumping of a low-flying helicopter approaching rapidly from the south sent him diving for cover behind a clump of tussock. Hamish was annoyed he had not heard it earlier and he stayed hidden as the chopper made a meticulous grid search of his immediate area, passing so close to him at one stage that he was blinded by grit and dust. Eventually it muscled its way farther to the north.

Hamish decided to abandon caution and jog in a straight line for the foothills. Forty-five minutes later he hit the snow line and began to climb. He knew that if he maintained a reasonably straight westerly ascent, he would have to eventually come to the mountain's traverse trail, and if he walked to the south, it would lead him to the Rangipo Hut, but a direct climb was no mean feat. The foothills looked smooth from the safety of State Highway 1, but up close they were a jumble of mini-mountains and deep gullies, and several times he lost his footing in the snow and tumbled into shallow crevasses. He was beginning to feel seriously cold.

By two o'clock, Hamish was in dogged automatic mode, slogging his way through increasingly thick snow, but despite the numbing cold, his mind was still firm and his direction sure. Eventually he realized that he had reached some sort of roughly horizontal ledge that had to be the trail. He now headed directly into the southerly and felt the full, brutal force of the wind. The snow took the definition off shapes, and several times Hamish walked right off the trail. Each haul back up was exhausting and time-consuming. The worst part was sleet and small rock particles slamming into his exposed face, but he dared not stop, not yet. There was still a long way to go before nightfall.

An eternity later, the wind suddenly eased and a black wall blocked Hamish's progress. He had almost walked directly into the north face of the Rangipo Hut. Despite his desperate need for shelter, Hamish did not enter the hut, because once inside, he knew he might not be able to leave, and this was the first place they would look for him. Just a brief rest sitting against the north-facing side would be okay, though, and he was keen to make another diary entry. He slid down the wall and sank into the snow.

## Diary Entry 3—July 31, 4:00 p.m.

This could be a short entry because my hands are so cold I can barely write. At least the overhang of the roof is keeping the book dry. I have renewed admiration for Robert Scott. How the hell he managed to keep writing his diary when he was in ten times worse condition than me is beyond belief. So I am going to stop feeling sorry for myself and just get on with it.

Firstly, this cold, it does interesting things to the body. I have read quite a lot about hypothermia and how the body and the mind react when they're in a hypothermic state. I will definitely be suffering from hypothermia in the not-too-distant future, so I will be able to analyze it firsthand, which is kind of strange. At what stage do I become incapable of studying my physical reactions because my mind is slipping? This is unique, cutting-edge research because what researcher in their right mind deliberately exposes themselves to mortal danger just to conduct interesting experiments? Possibly heaps, possibly just me. Next thing—am I in my right mind? Don't know. Lots of people think I have never been right in the head. Maybe they're on to something! Wow, big breakthrough, eh? I can almost see the smiles of glee— smartarse Hamish sees the light. No way, suckers! I'm right in the head for me, and that's all that matters. My hands and feet are now aching like hell, which is a good sign because it means the blood is still flowing freely to my extremities. It's when you lose feeling in your hands and feet that you know you are in serious trouble. This means the blood is retreating to protect my vital organs, and if I survive, it's likely I'll suffer some sort of permanent frostbite damage and will, at the least, lose one or two toes or fingers to gangrene. So, as you can see, I am still sharp as a tack to be writing all this good information.

To be honest, I am a bit scared—yes, that's right, scared. My plan is to climb Girdlestone Peak, and if you don't know, at 2,659 meters, that is almost as high as the top of Mount Ruapehu itself and considerably higher than Mount Egmont. It's a bit deceptive, though, because even low places on the Central Plateau are almost 1,000 meters above sea level. I've been doing a slow climb all the way to the hut, so I reckon I've got about 1,000 meters to go. It's not the cold and the climb that scare me, it's the "then what?" bit. It all seemed very clear when I was planning my trip back at New Horizons—I would climb to the top and die a hero. Or I would climb almost to the top and collapse, but be found by Mr. Wihongi. Together we would struggle up the last few meters, and then . . . That's right, it sounds childish, and probably is. I want people to remember me as a brave hero, not some mental misfit living in gaga land. Maybe it's meeting Trev that has changed things for me? When I said that I called my father Morris Minor, he said that compared to him, I had a dream father, and I should stop being a dork and show my dad the respect he deserves. Maybe. All I know is that I'm not turning back now. I've never been a quitter and I'm not about to become one now. Have to stop writing as I can barely hold my pen and it's getting hard even for me to decipher what I've written, let alone anyone who finds this diary. Into the storm once more. Hope I have the strength and guts to keep going. If ever I needed my heroes, it's right now. This may be my final entry but can't think of any clever final words, except "into the storm once more," and that's kind of clever-sounding.

Hamish

# 101 CHAPTER FOUR

Five men stood at the base of the snow line and stared up at the mountain in the fading afternoon light. Two dispirited dogs sheltered behind a large rock, shivering. Toko was shouting over the howling wind at two policemen and two army search and rescue specialists.

"I'm telling you, he's up there. The dogs have his scent right up to this point. Where else could he have gone?"

"No way, mate," replied one of the policemen. "The kid's fourteen, you say, and wearing stuff-all? He can't have made it this far, let alone climbed up to the bloody hut. The dogs lost his scent ages ago—it's you we've been following."

Toko remained silent. Len Pryer, the older of the two soldiers, moved to his shoulder.

"Come on, Toko. Think about it. He must have doubled back on us and returned to the highway. You said he's real clever and a student of military tactics, right? Okay, then, let's imagine that this is a genuine conflict scenario. He would not deliberately go into a no-win situation. It's suicidal madness to head up Girdlestone Peak in this weather. Come on, man, look at me! No kid, and definitely no soldier with half a brain, would consider climbing the mountain in this weather. You heard what the museum staff said, he looked totally normal and in control, and anyway, the chopper covered all this area before the weather closed in. We can't go any farther today. Shit, we've only got an hour of light left at the most. We just can't risk it."

"No! None of you are listening. You've all got to understand that this isn't a normal kid. If he sets his mind to do something, he follows through and does it. He is definitely up there and I've got to go after him."

Len stared at him in frustration. "For God's sake, man, you've got an arm in a cast. How the fuck are you going to climb through snow? This is all about what happened up here before, isn't it? This is still tough-as-teak Toko trying to prove something!"

"I dunno, could be part of it, but this is not some sort of self-healing redemption trip I'm on here. There is a fourteen-year-old boy up there somewhere with a death wish and we can't stand around arguing the toss. We have to keep going!"

"Stuff that! I'm giving you a direct order now, soldier. Turn around and start walking!"

"Good try, Len," Toko replied, "but I'm going. If you're not coming, then I suggest you head back now. In case you haven't noticed, it's getting bloody cold."

"Okay, okay, wait up, you stubborn bugger! What if you do find him? He'll be hypothermic for a start. Here, you're taking this survival gear, and don't rely on your bloody cell phone in this weather. I'm giving you a radio."

Len emptied his pack and began to systematically stuff Toko's pack with survival blankets, Swanndri jacket, wool balaclavas, gloves, a walkie-talkie radio and finally a thermos filled with hot, sweet coffee. He helped Toko lift the pack, then, with a frustrated grunt, headed off in the opposite direction and left him to find Hamish.

# 101

# CHAPTER
# FIVE

Hamish put his diary back inside his pack and tried to stand up. Nothing happened. He seemed to have split into two people. The physical Hamish was collapsed against the hut wall in an increasingly dangerous hypothermic state, while the intellectual Hamish was looking on with detached interest. The two were having some kind of dialogue.

"So this is what hypothermia's like. First the cold causes severe pain in the body's extremities to make sure the mind registers that urgent action is needed, then, if the mind doesn't, or can't, react to the situation, the blood begins to retreat to protect the vital organs and you feel a soothing numbness and extreme tiredness. Can't lie here, though. Get up, Hamish."

"Sorry, can't."

"Yes you can, you weakling. Get up now and walk!"

Hamish dragged himself to his feet and prepared to face the full blast of the wind. It was like a hammer blow to the head. He estimated that his ascent path to Girdlestone Peak was about half an hour to the southwest, but it was almost dark now and he began to doubt that he would get that far. It wouldn't be for lack of trying, though. He bent into the horizontal sleet and stumbled on through the raging storm.

The only indication Hamish had that he might have begun to climb was when he suddenly staggered backward. The realization that he had probably started the ascent of Girdlestone Peak sent a spurt of adrenaline through his exhausted body. He didn't really know how long it would take to get to the top, or even if it was possible. All that mattered now was moving forward and fighting the voices in his head that cried out for shelter and rest. So he went forward, one foot in front of the other. Mind still operating, but feet increasingly numb, a little like walking on stilts. On and on, stumbling, falling but getting up again to keep on going. Hamish's life narrowed to the progress of each step as he inched upward.

They weren't his feet, couldn't be. "Move, you bastards!" he commanded them. But eventually his legs refused to move and he sank into the snow.

Suddenly, a muscular young man with a shock of straw-colored hair shook Hamish's shoulder.

"It's a youth. Who are you, boy? Can you hear me? Hephaestion, bring skins and warm wine. Quickly, I think he's still alive."

The two men tilted Hamish's head back and poured a measure of the steaming liquid down his throat. He spluttered and retched the whole lot up again.

"Who are you? Are the Persians now reduced to sending boys to spy on Alexander?"

"I'm not a spy, Alexander. My name is Hamish Graham and I've got to get to the top of Girdlestone Peak before they find me."

"Don't lie to me, boy! I can tell by your eyes that you are lying. Did you know you have a slow blink rate, boy? That's right, I called you a boy because that's all you are. A silly little lying boy."

"No, I'm telling the truth. I'm on a mission of great importance and need to climb to the top of Girdlestone Peak."

"Well, you won't get far by lying on your back in the snow like a weakling. If, as you say, you have a mission to climb a certain peak, then that is good and admirable, but you must get to your feet and keep going."

"I can't. I think I'm dying."

"Ha! Listen to this, Hephaestion. The soft little fellow thinks he's dying. A mere six hours in the snow and he's dying. Six miserable hours in a minor blizzard and his skinny little legs have given up on him. Look at me, boy. I've been fighting for eight years and have been wounded twenty-two times. Do you see me giving up? Do you see me blabbering on about dying? I have been marching my army through these mountains for six weeks. Look around you, boy. I've got a hundred and fifty thousand people with me, including women and children. How many of them do you see lying on their backs like lazy slatterns, saying, 'I can't get up, I think I'm dying'? Come on, Hephaestion, we've wasted enough time on this loser. I want to find the pass before nightfall. He's of no possible use to us."

"No! Alexander, please don't leave me. I need your help. I want to die a noble death!" Hamish pleaded.

"I don't help gutless whelps, boy! Noble deaths are for those who have earned them. If you want to join my army and earn a noble death, you will get up now! If you can direct me to a pass down onto the plains, you will earn the right to ride with Alexander."

Hamish dragged himself to a sitting position but fell sideways.

"Just as I thought—too soft and too weak. I fight with men, not boys. Come, Hephaestion."

Hamish groaned in deep frustration as the two men vanished into the swirling snow and he collapsed backward in despair. It was so unfair. A sudden surge of white-hot anger forced him to his knees and then to his feet. He continued to climb, wooden legs driven by anger so intense he could smell it and taste it. But fifty meters later, his anger fizzled out, and once more Hamish pitched backward into the snow.

A deafening explosion, so close that rock fragments blasted his cheek, startled him. This was followed by the crackling of small arms fire, yells of pain and anger and then the sound of scrambling boots and falling masonry. A dust-streaked soldier peered through the acrid smoke.

"Captain Upham, have a look in here, sir, I think there's one still alive!" The familiar, walnut brown face of Charles Upham appeared over the pile of broken rubble.

"Yep, I think you're right, Corporal. It's a kid dressed in odd civvies. Who are you, cobber? Do you speak English?"

Relief flooded through Hamish. Surely Captain Charles Upham would be able to help him.

"Sir, I'm Hamish Graham from New Zealand and I've got to climb Girdlestone Peak. I don't want to die of hypothermia down here—I need your help to get to the top."

"Well, I suppose I could give a fellow comrade a hand, but what are you trying to prove by climbing this peak?"

"It's a challenge I have to complete. I . . . I have to get to the top because I don't fit in anywhere else and Mr. Wihongi was here with some army recruits who failed him. I am doing it for him."

"Shit oh dear—what a lot of palaver. Haven't got a clue what you're on about, boy. Are you sure you're right in the head? Are we meant to be impressed by your bravery? Do you want me to hold you aloft on some sort of bloody pedestal? Climbing this peak doesn't prove a damn thing to anybody. Sergeant Wihongi won't be impressed, you know. He thinks you're full of shit. He's told me all about you, cobber. He said, 'Charlie, that Hamish kid is just a joke. He goes on about toughness and valor, but when the pressure comes on, he deflates like a burst balloon, just like those other losers who couldn't hack it up here. You should have seen him during taiaha training. Couldn't even follow basic instructions. So weak he allows anger to pull him about like a rag doll. Oh yeah, wait until you hear this one, Charlie. The stupid little loser has this dumb plan to climb Girdlestone Peak, as if that proves something important.' Yep, that's what he told me about you, Hamish Graham. Hey, but I'm a decent bloke. I'm going to give you a simple test. If you can get up and follow me, you can join my platoon. Would you like that? Do you want to fight with Charles Upham?"

"Yes, yes, I do! That's what I want more than anything in the world. I want to join you, but I can't move my legs. Help me up, please!"

"No, mate, you've got to get up on your own steam. There's no room in my platoon for weaklings. I mean, how would you cope if we got hit by a gas attack? I reckon you would be the mug who couldn't get his mask on in time, and we have to get rid of deadwood like that. A Pommy chap called Wilfred Owen wrote a poem about weeding out the likes of you in the Great War. Go on, prove you're worthy of my help and get up!"

Hamish struggled to a sitting position, then a half crouch, and almost made it to his feet before collapsing yet again.

"You're no good to me, kid. No room for passengers. Fighting is work for men, not boys. See you later, cobber."

Without a backward glance, Upham shouldered his rifle and disappeared, leaving Hamish sobbing in the snow. He willed the anger to consume him again, but it only appeared as a flicker, an intangible sort of annoyance. It only managed to propel him ten or twenty meters before he crumpled and lay still once more.

A pungent odor filled his nostrils and then he was viciously yanked backward by the hair. A full *moko* framed a battle-hardened face.

"Too slow, boy. I have you now. Te Rauparaha, *e hoa,* over here! I have found a boy trying to escape."

A short muscular man approached and peered into Hamish's face.

"Huh, a Pakeha boy. What is a Pakeha boy doing fighting for these *kuri*?"

"I'm not fighting for anyone. My name is Hamish Graham and I have to climb Girdlestone Peak before they find me. Will you help me up?"

"Help you, boy? You are lying to me. I will kill you, not help you!"

An instant calmness overtook Hamish.

"Yes, kill me. I want to be killed by you, Te Rauparaha. Yes, I have been plotting and fighting against you with Ngati Te Aho. Take your mere and smash my skull. Yes, do it! Do it now!"

The gnarled old warrior drew his mere from his cloak. It was a mottled green, almost transparent on the edges.

He held it close to Hamish's head, just above the left ear. Te Rauparaha lifted his arm to strike, but the mere never fell.

"No, boy, you do not have the mana to be killed by Te Rauparaha. That is an honor for those who have fought bravely and lost. You have just lost. You can't even manage a little climb in the mountains. Look at all the clothes you've got on and your flash leather boots. Do you see my fighting men in leather boots? We travel and fight with the skin of our feet touching the earth. No, you are definitely not worthy of being killed by me. I will leave you to be killed by the worms; they are more your size."

"No, I want to die! I'm ready for it."

"No, you're not, you *kikiki* little fool. You see death as a glorious honor, and yes, it can be for the very old or for those who are truly ready. But you are a boy. Stop this foolish game of death. Get on with living, not with dying."

Desperation surged through Hamish and he fought to get to his feet.

"No, I want you to kill me. I am worthy of your mere. Come back, all of you. Come back, you bastards!" With the very last of his strength he lurched forward, perhaps ten meters, and then collapsed for the last time.

A strong arm lifted Hamish into a sitting position. He

struggled weakly and muttered through swollen lips, "Help me or kill me. Please . . . Alexander, Captain Upham, Te Rauparaha . . . I'm sorry, help me or kill me . . . I'm sorry, I can't go on."

Toko clutched the freezing boy close to his chest and wept with relief. Hamish roused himself enough to murmur "Help me or kill me" before surrendering to darkness again. Despite his own exhaustion, Toko drew on deep reserves of strength. He wrapped Hamish in a survival blanket and pulled a thick balaclava over the boy's head. Toko then slowly hoisted Hamish in an awkward fireman's lift and started the long process of carrying him back down the slope. How the boy had made it more than halfway up the peak, he would never know, and if he hadn't heard Hamish's bizarre rantings coming from above, he would certainly not have searched this high up the slope. The boy's life hung in the balance and he knew that if he didn't get to the hut within an hour, he would lose him. The enormity of that was just too much to contemplate.

# 101

# CHAPTER
# SIX

Disaster struck a mere fifty meters from the hut. Toko had stopped to reposition the boy on his aching shoulders when suddenly the portion of trail they were on sheered off and began a looping plummet into the darkness below. Toko threw himself and Hamish backward, but it was too late and they followed the collapsing rock and snow over the ledge. They fell about twenty meters but miraculously landed in thick snow in a bowl-like depression on the very edge of a deep crevasse, from which there would have been no chance of survival. They appeared relatively unscathed and had even landed in an area totally protected from the deadly wind. Toko positioned his flashlight on a ledge, then ripped off Hamish's polar fleece and replaced it with Len's heavy-duty Swanndri jacket. He also pulled a second thick balaclava over Hamish's head and replaced his sodden gloves with dry ones. He even managed to get a little hot fluid into him before rewrapping him in the survival blanket. When nothing more could be done to keep Hamish alive, he began the urgent task of attempting to make phone or radio contact with Len at the army base. The storm still raged above and the cell phone was dead. The walkie-talkie had life, but the depression they were in blocked coverage and he needed to get back up to the trail to enable a direct line with base. Nothing for it but to stuff the radio inside his jacket and try to climb back up.

Twenty minutes later Toko had to admit defeat. He just couldn't climb the rock face one-handed. There was only one solution. Cut off the plaster cast holding his shattered arm in place. His old army knife had a strong serrated blade, and a few minutes later he shook the cast free. The pain was intense and immediate, but this was not important. On the second climb he achieved better balance and a partial grip with his left hand. Slowly but surely he clawed his way to the top and eventually rolled over the jagged edge to lie on the trail fighting for breath.

He heard running sounds and then a flashlight stabbed at his eyes, immediately followed by a vicious kick to the ribs. The next kick was aimed at his face, but Toko rolled away just in time and managed to lash out blindly with his left foot, catching his attacker on the knee and giving him just enough time to scramble to his feet before he was smashed heavily to the ground. The shattered arm took the full impact of the charge and a black void smothered Toko's screams of pain.

A series of hard slaps dragged him back into consciousness. He was propped against the sheltered side of the hut, hands bound behind his back.

"Come on, you bastard, wake up! You and me have got some business to take care of."

Toko spat blood and phlegm onto the snow. The howling of the wind distorted his attacker's voice, but he instantly recognized the face peering into his own.

"Victor. You came after me. Thought you would, but not quite so soon. How did you get here?"

"Yeah, that's right. Get me talking, play for time. Won't do you any good, though." Victor had to shout to be heard. "I'm calling the shots now, just like you were when you killed my brother Charlie. After our little chat, I got Terry to show me Hamish's letter. I knew where you'd be going anyway because Uncle Sid came down to find the spot where you'd killed his nephew. One of us was always going to get you. With all the fuss over Hamish, and you going after him, no one saw me take Mr. Whittle's old Land Rover—yeah, learned some good skills in Auckland. Whittle's a tramper and he had all the gear I needed, same size as me too. Love to see his face when he finds his baby gone! I just drove on down. You guys went through the Desert Road barrier a few minutes before me. I could see your lights. I put Whittle's bull bars to good use and smashed through the barrier. I pulled off the road and used his binoculars to watch those army guys and dogs returning, then put the truck to the test. Got it to within a hundred meters of where I figured you'd started the climb. It's a bit stuffed now, though, just like you, eh, Wihongi!"

The utter craziness of the situation brought a weary smile to Toko's face.

"But the cold and the climb . . . how did you—"

"What about it? I've been on pig hunts tougher than this when I was just a kid! I dealt with it and now I'm here and I'm calling the shots, so shut up!"

"Victor, listen. We can sort this out, not now, though. I found Hamish, but we fell off the trail where you found me. He's in a really bad way, advanced hypothermia. You've got to help me to make radio contact with Waiouru and then get him back to the hut before he dies. Quick, get these ropes off me."

Victor leaned close and shouted into Toko's face.

"No, you listen, big tough Maori *fulla*! I really thought you were the man, the real thing, but all the time you were the one who led Charlie to his death. Jeez, you're lucky Uncle Sid never found out. Did you think telling me would make it okay? Maybe if you'd told me right at the start, I could have lived with it, but all the time you had us kids licking your arse, thinking how cool and tough you were, and all that time you just lapped it up— good old Matua Toko. "Be like me, boys. Be a big, tough, law-abiding man like me." And when you blocked Hamish's taiaha, here's dumb old me thinking it was because you were trying to save my life, but now I know. You were just trying to save your own life. You thought saving me would wipe your debt to Charlie. All that 'Victor, get some baling twine from the shed and secure my arm' heroic shit. And that utu performance you put on for the boys. I'll show you fucking utu." Victor kicked out at Toko's damaged arm and was rewarded with a gasp of pain.

"Don't talk bullshit, Victor! Yes, I should have told you earlier, but I didn't because I knew this is how you would probably react. I'm not denying that your brother's death is my responsibility alone and you have the right to hate me at this time. But if we don't act right now, there will be another dead boy on these mountains. If you can help me to get Hamish inside this hut, I promise you I will lead you to the exact spot Charlie died and you can do whatever it is you think you have to do."

"No, you're going to take me there right now. Come on, get up!"

Victor dragged Toko to his feet and propelled him back into the face of the southerly.

A few minutes later Toko stopped.

"We're here. Stop pushing me, we're at the spot."

"You're lying, Wihongi, keep going."

"No, Victor, I'm not lying. The boys fell when they were almost at the hut, in almost the exact spot where Hamish and I fell."

"Don't give me that crap! Take me to the right place. It has to be where Charlie died."

"Listen, Victor, it's too dark to see now, but Hamish and I fell into a kind of bowl beside a deep crevasse. Your brother and his mate weren't so lucky. They fell right in. I had to climb down almost a hundred meters to where Charlie landed. He didn't have a chance. So come on. What are you going to do? Push me off? Then what? What are you going to do about Hamish?"

"He's not my problem—you are!"

Toko walked to a certain spot five meters on and stood

facing Victor on the very edge of the crumbling rock face. He swayed in the wind but noted that it was abating a little.

"Okay, Victor, I'm ready. Come and push me off."

"Shut up! I'll do it when I'm ready."

"Yeah, thought so. When it comes to the crunch, you cave in."

"Turn around!"

"You can't do it, eh, boy? You don't have the guts to look me in the face and do it. You're just like your brother."

"You shut your fucking mouth! You don't know anything about Charlie. I'm going to kill you, you bastard!" But Victor still didn't move.

A sneer filled Toko's face. "Yeah, just like little Charlie, all full of shit and—"

Victor screamed in anguish as he charged straight at his tormentor. Toko moved back with the charge and spun to his left at the same time, ensuring that Victor plunged into the darkness with him.

Toko's estimations were only marginally out and they crashed into deep snow, inches from the edge of the crevasse and almost within touching distance of Hamish.

Both were winded, but the miracle had repeated itself and apart from further damage to Toko's arm, they were unhurt. He staggered to a kneeling position. "Victor, you need to untie my hands. Come on, man, untie me!"

Victor lay prone, shocked sobs engulfing his shaking body.

"Come on. Get up, boy. You did well, but don't give up on me now. You have to be strong. I didn't mean any of those things. I had to say them to get you to push me over at this exact spot, because saving Hamish is all up to you now. And yes, this is the spot where Charlie fell. A meter to the right and we would have joined him."

Victor roused himself to a sitting position and clutched his knees. He wiped a hand over his snotty nose and spat into the snow, then shuffled to the very edge of the prec-ipice and stared into the darkness below. "I'm sorry, Char-lie, I've let you down. I'm just useless to everyone."

Toko kept his voice quiet and matter-of-fact. "You've let no one down, Victor. You did all you had to do and more. Charlie is very proud of you. I'm proud of you. What you did took huge guts. But what you have to do now is untie my hands so we can get Hamish up to the hut. There's a knife on my belt; that'll be quicker. I need you to cut the rope."

Victor looked at Toko, then pulled the knife from the leather sheath on his belt. He pulled out the long blade and stared at it. Toko turned his back to him and waited.

Victor made a violent slash and the rope fell from Toko's wrists.

"That's it. Good man, Victor. Now we have to help Hamish. Look at him! Look at your mate, Hamish. What would Charlie want, eh? Would he want you to give in or would he want you to be strong and save a life? I think you know the answer to that."

Holding the knife, Victor faced Toko and threw it into the darkness. He walked to the edge of the crevasse and flopped onto the snow.

Toko slowly moved closer, but not close enough to stop Victor's sudden lunge. Toko snaked out his good arm, just managing to grab the collar of Victor's jacket as, with an animal yell, the boy disappeared over the side. His grip was firm, but Victor weighed almost eighty kilograms and was slowly pulling Toko over the edge with him.

Noises and voices pulling and pushing, looming shapes and dark lurid smells, hands holding, clutching and grasping, refusing to let go, smothering and suffocating.

Hamish snapped into consciousness, gasping for breath. His mind alive but his body heavy and dull. He shook his head to free himself from the insistent voices, but they wouldn't vanish—in fact, they were very close to him.

". . . I'm just useless . . . Charlie is very proud of you . . . get Hamish up to the hut . . . I think you know the answer . . ." There was a scream and then a different-sounding voice, a terrified voice. "Don't let go . . . please, oh Jesus, pull me up."

Toko's voice sounded out. "Victor, stop struggling and fold your arms so your jacket stays on. I've got you; everything's going to be all right."

Hamish groaned loud enough to be heard over the wind.

"Hamish? You're conscious? Thank Christ! Can you move at all? If you can, I need you right now. Listen carefully. I'm holding on to Victor—he's hanging over the edge of the crevasse and he's pulling me over with him. I can't hold ground much longer. You need to help me—lie over my legs to give me some lifting power. Do it now!"

Another voice, high and strangled. "Hamish, come on, man! Help!"

This was crazy. Hamish thought he'd heard Mr. Wihongi saying something absurd about Victor. He could hear Victor's voice as well. Mind tricks, just like his hallucinations up the mountain. He decided to surrender to the comparative sanity of darkness and closed his eyes.

Shouting in agony, Toko used his damaged arm to hurl a handful of snow directly into Hamish's face. He came to with a start and stared in shock at the bizarre, half-lit scene. A man was lying facedown in the snow, leaning over the edge of a cliff holding something that looked very heavy.

"Hamish. Listen carefully. It's me, Toko Wihongi. I found you on the mountain, but we fell off the trail just before we got back to the hut. Victor came after me and he's now over the edge—I can't hold him forever. If ever there was a time for you to be a hero, it's right now. Unless you can help me, both Victor and I will certainly fall to our deaths. This is not a dream or a game—this is the real world. Don't ask questions. I know you can do it. Do you understand what I'm saying?"

Hamish nodded and, using all his willpower, tried to pull himself to a kneeling position. He collapsed backward.

"Get the blanket off first. Focus, Hamish! Try rolling toward me or pushing yourself backward. I need you to lie over my legs. Come on, boy. Do it! Fight for me!"

Fight—a familiar word. A flicker of anger began to burn in Hamish. Shame and humiliation joined the mix until the flame took hold. "My body will not do this to me; I am stronger than this. Move, you useless sack of shit!" He began to shuffle on his back toward the edge of the crevasse, toward the voice. When he was close, he lifted himself to his hands and knees, then collapsed over Toko's legs.

Now that he had stopped inching toward the edge, Toko used every remaining gram of strength to try and pull Victor back up over the edge. But the boy was too heavy and Toko's arm felt like lead. There was simply no way he was going to be able to pull the boy up over the edge. He groaned in helpless rage.

"Hamish . . . can't do it . . . hand's going numb . . . can't hold on much longer. Roll off my legs and let us go. Go on, roll off. You might be able to save yourself. Listen . . . the wind's easing up there. Searchers will be coming with first light. The hut is just off to the right. You have to stay conscious, though. This is what you have to do. Go on . . . roll off."

Hamish felt his anger grow taste and smell. He nurtured it until he felt its white tendrils fork through his body. All this, all of it, was his fault. And only he could make it right. He found his voice for the first time, although his throat was on fire and the words were slurred and torturous.

"Mr. Wihongi, I'm not going to let you go over the

edge. Just don't let go. Is my pack still with me? I've got some rope and we can use it to pull Victor up. Tell me what to do."

A flicker of hope.

"Yes, I should have thought of that. Your pack's there, beside mine. We need more light too. If you've got a flashlight, bring that as well. I need you to roll off me very slowly. Make sure I don't start to move, though. Push my boots as deep into the snow as you can. I need you to make a slipknot in one end of the rope, you know, like a cowboy's knot. Can you make that?"

"Of course I can, I'm not stu— Yes, I can make a slipknot. Don't know if I can make my hands work, but I'll try."

He shuffled back to the pack and fished out the rope and flashlight. He used his teeth to pull off Toko's thick gloves and was glad to feel immediate needles of pain. With drunken movements, he eventually made a service-able sliding noose at one end of the rope. Flashlight in mouth and gloves back on, Hamish slithered back to Toko's side.

"Okay, Hamish, you need to half lie on me to stop me moving, then lower the noose over the side and try and put it around one of Victor's legs. Victor? Are you follow-ing this? Hamish is going to slip a rope over your foot.

It's like a hangman's noose. You're going to lift your foot, grab the rope and work it up over your other leg and around your waist. You must make sure the knot is secure enough to hold all your weight. Speak, boy! Are you following all this?"

"Yes, yes—just hurry." Victor's voice echoed up from inside the crevasse.

It was infuriating. Victor was only a couple of meters away, but strong updraft winds kept blowing the rope away from his legs. Eventually, more by chance than skill, the rope slipped over one of Victor's boots and he soon had it worked up to his waist. Hamish began to pull the rope tight to take a little of the strain. Toko's next order was more urgent.

"I'm losing the grip. Quick, Hamish, secure the rope. Move, I can't hold him!"

Hamish lurched up on his wobbly, numb legs and tied the rope around his waist as he staggered back to the rock face. He barely had time to throw himself behind an angular rock protruding from the cliff face when Toko lost his grip and Victor's full weight snapped the rope tight. Hamish was slammed into the rock, but he was firmly wedged behind it. Toko had time to regain some of the power in his good arm and he started pulling at the rope. With Toko's help, Victor scrambled up the side of the crevasse and soon lay sprawled and gasping at Toko's feet.

## Diary Entry 4—August 1, 8:00 a.m.

We are waiting for the rescue team to arrive and take us to Waiouru Base Hospital. Well, I'm waiting. Mr. Wihongi and Victor are sleeping. As you can see by my writing, I don't have much feeling in my right hand, so this will be a really short entry with no sidetracking. Mr. Wihongi thinks I will probably lose a finger or two. Serves me right, you reckon. Yeah, perhaps. Doesn't worry me too much if I lose the odd finger or toe. Scars of battle. I feel bad about dragging Mr. Wihongi and Victor into all this, but Victor said that without me, they would have died. Bullshit, without me they never would have been in this situation in the first place. I'm a hero—yeah right! He's the hero. And Victor maybe. What I did wasn't heroic, but even my hordes of detractors will have to admit it was ballsy, if you know what I mean. I can't say too much about why I tried to climb up that peak. It seems a bit like it happened to someone else a long time ago. And I'm not going to say much about what happened when we arrived back at the hut because that's private territory. All I'll say is that we sorted a few things out.

Hamish

## Diary Entry 5—August 7, 9:00 a.m.

I don't know whether to call this a diary entry or a journal entry. I'm on my laptop of course, but it feels more like a diary so I'll call it that. Probably a bit of both, really. Whatever it is, I think I'll just write one more entry and e-mail it up to New Horizons for Mrs. Grenville and the staff to read—if they want to, that is. I'm guessing they will because their lives are probably very dull without me to spark it up for them.

I have had several days to think things over now. Mr. Wihongi said I was as close to death as anyone could be when he found me in the snowstorm. He was stunned that I had almost made it to the top, dressed as I was and in those weather conditions. I was passing in and out of consciousness and yelling out crazy stuff like, "Kill me, I don't deserve to live." And, "Alexander, take me with you—give me a chance." Very embarrassing. It was crazy how real those hallucinations were. They were as real to me at the time as my current reality of typing these words. I have read that several North and Central American Indian tribes frequently used cactus and mushroom based hallucinogenic drugs to enable them to experience alternate realities and I will definitely file this away for more thought and research.

A helicopter flew in next morning and took us to the

hospital at the Waiouru Army Base, and although hospitals are weird places mostly, and best avoided, I can recommend this one. Ultra-functional place—a bit like the museum. Victor and Mr. Wihongi were discharged after two days, but my injuries were the worst, and I have been here now for almost a week. The doctor said that my hypothermia took several days to stabilize but that I am not out of danger yet. Three of my toes and two of my fingers are still quite dark and if the blood doesn't begin to circulate soon, I will lose them. Doesn't worry me, though. As I said before—scars of battle.

Yesterday they were going to fly me to Wellington Hospital to be nearer my parents, but I made a big stink and they seem to be able to have me here now for a bit longer.

The only people I would let near me for a while were Mr. Wihongi and Victor. It's weird about Victor really, because here's a guy I've tried to wipe out several times, but he doesn't seem to care. When he was first allowed to see me in the critical care unit he wanted to hongi me, like I was his best mate! Yeah, Victor's all right. He and Mr. Wihongi are cool about each other as well, but I don't think they can ever be close. They have obviously come to some sort of understanding about

Charlie, but I think his ghost will always fill the space between them. Seems I might have been a bit hard on Mr. Whittle. Turns out he doesn't want to press charges over Victor taking his Land Rover. This could have something to do with the insurance company accepting that it was written off in Victor's little test drive to the mountain, but whatever the reason, thanks, Mr. Whittle. Perhaps, just perhaps, I underestimated you. Victor is being released to the care of his family in Tolaga Bay and he is going to return to school in Gisborne. He will move in with his grandmother for a while and he's really keen for me to come and see where he lives. He said there are some cool pa sites for me to check out and a big wild boar with my name on it. I'm going to do the sticking part and I can almost feel the hot blood spilling over my hands. Bring it on!

I was relieved that Mr. Wihongi was at least a bit pissed off about what I did. Jeez, I need someone to have a go at me! But he was kind of proud too, I think. He said that if I didn't let my parents come and see me, then I could kiss good-bye to him as well. So yesterday I saw them, and it was kind of good, really, although Mum cried quite a lot and made far too much noise. She only stopped when I reminded her that we were in a military hospital and that certain standards of behavior were required of visitors. Dad was a little better, although he didn't know whether to hug me or shake my hand, so he kind of did a lame combination of the two. He said that he and Mum were looking forward to having me come home, and I feel kind of good about that. I bet the neighbors are missing me as well! The Youth Court said that I just have to serve out my original time. Don't know how I feel about this. Surely I should be punished in some way for escaping and then taking off into the mountains, causing all sorts of hassles for lots of people? Mr. Wihongi and Victor almost died because of me. Don't get me started again on the justice system in our PC mad country. People my age are virtually untouchable. I say bring back public flogging and being clamped in stocks in public squares. Anyway, as usual I don't have any say in the matter and my original time stands. A condition of all this is that I spend a lot more time with Terry to try and work through "my issues." He's coming down tomorrow to see me and we're going to start my therapy straightaway. Whatever—I can play this game a bit more, I suppose, and working with him is hardly a punishment. As long as they don't expect me to eat humble pie and pretend I've seen the light and promise to be a good boy forevermore. Don't know about you, but I hate it when some ex-loser type stands up and goes on about having some sort of stupid epiphany experience and now they just want to help young people to reach their potential. The best part about having to work with Terry is that I can help him too, because to be honest, he's too soft on the boys and might benefit from some of my ideas on how to deal with bad kids. I have decided to spend my last month helping him to learn how to be a successful counselor for out-of-it boys. I have been thinking a lot about this already and have a whole program just waiting to go, and if you have read my first journal entry, you will have an idea what it will be like. Terry will become famous as the instigator of a whole new branch of therapy for tough kids. I'm not into blowing my own trumpet, but they could do worse than name these new techniques after me—the Graham Method.

So only a month to go. But I suppose the boys' home just wouldn't be the same without Mr. Wihongi there. Yeah, that's right, he's decided to give the army another shot. It must have been my amazing powers of persuasion. We have had several long talks while I've been recuperating and he thinks that we have both had a chance to tell our demons to bugger off! He is keen to serve abroad and has been talking about East Timor or Afghanistan.

He told me he is still really worried about my state of mind, especially my obsession with my main men (you know who!), but I told him this morning that I was never really obsessed with them at all and that even if I had been just a little besotted (great word, thanks, Terry!), I feel a bit differently about them now. It wasn't any of them who saved me—in fact, you could say they were downright useless! It was all down to my real hero! Mr. Wihongi said that the last thing he wanted was for me to "put him on some sort of bloody pedestal." It was a bit spooky, him using similar words to Upham, but I reckon they are very similar men, and I wouldn't be at all surprised if Mr. Wihongi earns himself a VC one day. Afghanistan seems a likely place for a Kiwi soldier to earn one. I can just see Mr. Wihongi braving enemy fire to save fallen comrades and then being all humble and shy when his bravery is rewarded. Anyway, he keeps on saying I have to put the past into perspective and live for the future. I think he's right. After all, I'm fifteen soon—I'm not a kid anymore.

I had one more visitor yesterday. Trev Mitchell called in on the way back from the drag racing in Upper Hutt. When I hadn't called him by six o'clock that night, he did ring the police. They knew I was missing by then, although they were glad to find out how I got to Waiouru so quickly. Apparently they gave him a bit of a roasting about dropping a fourteen-year-old absconder on the side of a road in a southerly storm and were considering charging him with aiding and abetting an escaper. He must have talked them around, or maybe Mr. Wihongi put in a few good words for him.

Trev was amazed at what I had done, but he said it was high time I "stopped fartin' around doing drongo stuff!" He wants me to go back to school and then go to university. He said he would have loved to study some sort of engineering and that he would kick my butt if I ended up wasting as many years as him. I reckon he hasn't wasted a moment. His dragster took out the top overall speed prize at the Upper Hutt races and he built the whole thing himself, including lots of the engine parts. I know a bit about rocket propulsion, and he's real keen for me to come and stay with him for a week or so, to help him design a rocket-propelled drag car. He's got this plan to build a drag motor that uses ammonium perchlorate as a propellant, just like a real rocket. Sounds way cool! Trev said the conditions of me coming to stay with him are that my parents have to agree, I have to be attending a high school and my visit has to be in the school holidays. This is quite depressing actually, because unless school has changed radically in the last few months, I know I still won't fit in. I don't want you to get to the end of my last diary entry and get all misty eyed on me thinking that Hamish has turned a corner and will ride into the sunset and live happily ever after. If I want to go up and see Trev, it will be because I decide I want to see him again, not because I have been a good little boy sucking up to stupid teachers. Oh yeah, Trev also said that there was only one vehicle faster than his at the meet and that was a heavily adapted Ducati motorbike, rebuilt on the same lines as old Burt Munro's Indian motorbike. He ended up being real friendly with the rider, a bloke called Neil, who he reckoned was some sort of gang leader from an outfit in Upper Hutt called Rommel's Raiders. Good one, Neil!

So this is the end of my diary/journal. If you liked it, good; if you didn't, I don't give a toss. For what it's worth, I really hope I can get on top of the anger. Mind you, it was anger that got me fired up enough to get Victor out of the crevasse. Maybe it's not the anger, but how it's used. Anyway, shouldn't be too much of a problem for me—life's all about choices.

Hamish

# GLOSSARY

## NEW ZEALAND ENGLISH TERMS

**Anzac** *(Australian and New Zealand Army Corps)* **Day** – a national day of remembrance in both New Zealand and Australia. During World War I, Australian and New Zealand troops landed at Gallipoli (Turkey) on April 25, 1915. This was a tactical error on the part of the British commanders (they sent the troops to the wrong landing spot), and the Australians and New Zealand troops were decimated. Anzac Day is a day of remembrance for the troops lost in all the wars in which New Zealand and Australia have fought.

**-as** – *big-as, rugged-as, sweet-as*: a New Zealand colloquial/slang term mostly used by young people as an unfinished simile

**bar** – as in "didn't want a bar of it" – didn't want anything to do with it

**bob** – originally a slang term for a British shilling, now a disappearing colloquialism referring to small change

**borstal** – reformatory

**bull bars** – strong metal bars or metal frames attached to the front of a vehicle to prevent injury to passengers if livestock were hit on the road

**bushcraft** – knowledge of how to live and survive in the bush (wilderness)

**caravan** – trailer, mobile home

**cobber** – buddy

**crumping** – a term originally from Los Angeles that refers to a style of dancing popular on the rap scene, a mix of dance and stylized fight moves

**Desert Road, the** – a bleak stretch of the main highway of New Zealand's North Island that runs through Tongariro National Park

**doss** – to sleep or bed down in a convenient place; usually used with *down*

**drongo** – idiot

**fag** – cigarette

**frighteners** – as in "put the frighteners up"—put a scare into

**get done/got done** – get caught, get arrested

**gum boot** – a rubber boot

**hardout** – hard-core

**loo** – toilet

**lounge** – living room

**Matron** – a woman at a boarding school in charge of ensuring that the sleeping dormitories are in order; she also has a motherly role

**Morris Minor** – a type of British car manufactured through the 1950's and 60's, vaguely similar to a Volkswagen Beetle

**nick** – steal

**on-to-it** – with it; socially or culturally up-to-date

**out-of-it** – in a dazed or confused state

**patched gang member** – a New Zealand gang member who has "earned" a patch; each gang has a separate patch design worn on the back of their jackets. A gang member usually earns a patch by doing something violently illegal. Leaving the gang is "dropping the patch."

**pinch** – steal

**Pom/Pommy** – Briton; especially an English immigrant

**practical math** – math that relates to real-life situations as opposed to an academic math course; practical math is sometimes for kids with lesser abilities

**psyching at me/psyched out** – freaking out/freaked out

**sachet** – a small bag or packet

**slattern** – an untidy, slovenly woman; also a slut or prostitute

**smoko** – morning or afternoon tea; traditionally workers were allowed to break for a cigarette, or "smoke"

**stroppy** – touchy, belligerent

**stubbies shorts** – short pants made of cotton or canvas material

**stuff or stuffed** – tired (being stuffed); mucked things up (stuffed up her life); screw (stuff that); not very much (wearing stuff-all, ate stuff-all); broken (stuffed lawn mowers)

**Swanndri** – a brand of outdoor clothing popular with hikers, farmers, and anyone else who works outside

**tappets** – small lever-type engine parts needing frequent adjustment in older cars for correct engine timing

**tea** – refreshments, usually including tea with sandwiches, crackers or cookies served in late afternoon, or a reception, snack or meal at which tea is served

**toss, arguing the** – arguing the point

**tucker** – food

**tramp/tramping/tramper** – hike/hiking/outdoorsman

**tussock** – a compact tuft, especially of grass or sedge; also an area of raised solid ground in a marsh or bog that is bound together by roots of low vegetation

**warder** – warden, prison guard


## MAORI TERMS

**e hoa** – friend, buddy

**haka** – traditional war dance/challenge

**hongi** – traditional greeting where noses are pressed together, still commonly used today

**iwi** – tribe

**kai** – food

**karakia** – prayer or chant for a specific occasion, such as a welcome or before a meal

**Karo waewae pourua** – command to leap forward and attack with a killing blow. Most *taiaha* work is done in a semi-crouch in preparation for sudden and dramatic leaps forward to catch opponents unaware.

**kauri** – any of various trees of the araucaria family; especially a tall timber tree of New Zealand having fine white straight-grained wood, also called *kauri pine*

**kikiki** – stupid idiot, childish idiot

**kinaki** – savory relish/tidbit/meat at meal

**kuri** – dog

**mana** – broadly the power of the elemental forces of nature embodied in an object or person or moral authority; also a person, or group of people, of great personal prestige and character

**Mangopare** – command to hold the taiaha up in a two-handed horizontal move so as to block a downward blow

**Maori** – Polynesian people native to New Zealand; also the Polynesian language of the Maori people

**Matua** – a term of respect similar to *uncle*

**Maui Potiki** – a well-known Maori mythical figure of legend

**mere** – a short fat club made from whalebone or greenstone

**moko** – traditionally a facial tattoo worn by warriors

**Ngati** – refers to an *iwi* or tribe. All of the different tribes throughout New Zealand traditionally have their own areas, and Maori still identify themselves by tribal affiliation, for example, "I am Ngati Porou."

**nga whatu** – literally "the eyes"; traditional taiaha had eye notches cut into the spear face and were often decorated with paua shell inserts

**Oz** – a slang term for Australia

**pa** – stockaded village

**Pakeha** – a person who is not of Maori descent; especially a white person

**patu** – weapon

**porangi** – crazy

**Poua upoko** – command to swing the taiaha over the head in a sweeping blow

**puku** – abdomen, stomach

**rangatira** – chief

**taiaha** – a long spear/club; like other important inanimate objects (houses, for instance), its parts were given human or lifelike physical characteristics

**taonga** – treasure

**taua** – a raiding party

**te arero** – literally "the tongue"; the spear or tongue-shaped top end of the taiaha

**te ate** – literally "the heart"; the part of the taiaha where the main life force resides

**te awe** – literally "the feather"; attached to the taiaha, symbolic of hair

**te rau** – literally "the legs"; the end part of the trunk of the taiaha, usually symbolized by a sprig of leaves tied to the end of the spear shaft

**te tinana** – literally "the body" or trunk of the taiaha

**te upoko** – literally "the top of the head"

**tino pai** – well done, good

**utu** – revenge

**wairua** – spirit

**Werohia** – command to stab or spear

**whanau** – family

### NEW ZEALAND SCHOOL SYSTEM:

New Zealand children start primary school (Years 1 through 6) at age five; Year 1 is comparable to kindergarten. Primary school is followed by two years (Years 7 and 8) at an intermediate school, then five years of high school (also referred to as "college") (Years 9, 10, 11, 12, and 13). Year 13 in New Zealand is the equivalent of twelfth grade in the United States.

All schools start their year the first week of February and end the year at Christmas (the long holidays are over the summer months of December and January).

Kids can leave school as early as the end of Year 11, when

they are sixteen years old, which is their first year of nationally assessed exams.

**THE SETTING:**

Most of the book's pivotal moments take place in Tongariro National Park, in the central part of New Zealand's North Island. This is a bleak area, popular with skiers and hikers, and is also the location of the army base at Waiouru. Three large volcanic mountains (dormant, not extinct!) are in this area— Ruapehu, Ngauruhoe and Tongariro. The eastern slopes of Ruapehu are where the story climaxes.